HER INDEPENDENCE DAY

A MILITARY REVERSE HAREM ROMANCE

K.C. CROWNE

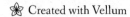

DESCRIPTION

Four strapping Marines are home for Independence Day.
And all four brothers in arms have their eyes on one lucky lady.

I moved in with my older brother after leaving a toxic relationship.
To my surprise he'll be going away for business...
Leaving me alone with four of his insanely HOT military best friends.

I remember drooling over them growing up.
Now they can't keep their eyes off me.

I must be imagining it, right?
How can all four want me?

One night, they sneak into my room,
Shirts off, their hands on my skin.
My heart racing a million miles a minute.

Will this be the most unforgettable night ever?
Or, will I regret letting my inhibitions finally get the best of me?
A full-length standalone reverse harem, age-gap romance. Each book in this series can be read on its own. All books come with an oh so satisfying happily ever after. No cheating or cliffhanger!

CHAPTER 1

WINONA

"I'm going to fucking *kill* him."

My brother crouches down in front of me and lays the cold compress he just purchased on my swollen eye. It stings like a bitch, but I'm so exhausted, drained, and cried out that I can't do much more than wince.

I'm seated on the curb of a gas station, my knees tucked to my chest as the heavy scent of gasoline and windshield wiper fluid fills my nose. The duffle bag beside me is full of all the clothes I managed to cram in while Chet wasn't looking, though I'm sure I left more than a few things behind in my haste. I thank my lucky stars it's warm out. I left in such a hurry, I had no time to think about changing, so I'm dressed in nothing but a pair of jean shorts and a thin grey shirt. I don't even have a jacket with me.

The passing June breeze brings with it the sound of distant traffic and the chirp of evening crickets from the surrounding woods, but it does little to soothe the trembling of my hands.

Don't you dare walk away from me, Winona!

William sighs, gently grasping my chin to get a better look at my face. His brows are pinched together in a steep frown, his lip curled up in a sneer. I don't think I've ever seen him more murderous.

"I'm so sorry," he says gently, which surprises me. "You should have told me things were so bad. Has Chet hit you before and you didn't tell me?"

I shake my head quickly. "No, this is... Things just got a little heated."

"What were you fighting about?" my brother asks as he takes a seat on the curb beside me.

He's dressed in a suit, his tie hanging loose, the top button undone. His light brown hair is windswept, and his forehead is a little sweaty. If I had to guess, I'd say he dropped everything to meet me here.

"I told him I was going to New York City in the fall," I mumble softly. "I got an interview to intern at Sterling Publishing House to work with a junior editor. They said they were really keen on meeting me because I was one of their top candidates."

William's eyes widen in delighted surprise. He bumps his knee against mine. "Seriously? Win, that's *great*. You've wanted to work in publishing since you were old enough to know what books were."

I cast my one good eye down to the pavement beneath my dirty shoes. After our fight, I waited until Chet passed out on the couch after a handful of beers before sneaking out of our apartment. I would have taken the keys to the car, but I was afraid they'd make too much noise and wake him. Besides, the car is technically in his name, and I wouldn't put it past Chet to call the cops on me for stealing his vehicle. Hell, even the apartment is in his name, so it's not like I could have kicked him out.

At the time, he insisted it was for my sake. He'd take care of everything. The bills, the car, our home, our finances... I'd felt cherished and cared for. Who doesn't want a man who knows how to provide? In hindsight, I realize how stupid that was. Naïve. I didn't realize until it was too late that Chet had trapped me, and I don't think I'll ever stop kicking myself for it.

You're nothing without me, do you understand?

I chew on the inside of my cheek. "Chet didn't think it was so great. When I told him I would be gone for four months, he lost it." My eyes burn with the threat of tears as the memories rush back. My swollen eye hurts twice as much. "We went back and forth. The argument got out of control, and before I knew what was happening, he..." My voice wobbles and my throat tightens. I can't bring myself to finish my sentence.

It all happened so fast. Chet and I argue from time to time, but fights happen. Just never like *this*. This one escalated from pointed words to harsh shoves, and then a closed fist careening toward my face. He hit me hard enough to knock me to the kitchen floor. I wanted to fight back, to not curl up in a ball and give up, but I was so shocked and blindsided I couldn't control my body.

Fuck, Winona, I'm so sorry. I didn't mean it. Are you okay? I love you, I love you.

Needless to say, he's never going to hurt me again because we're done. Like my mother always used to say: a man who'd dare raise a hand to you is bound to do it again and again and again. I've made a lot of stupid mistakes where Chet is concerned, but staying with him after the shit he just pulled? Out of the question.

William gingerly throws his arm over my shoulder and gives me a side hug. "What do you need, Win? Anything at all. Just name it. I'm assuming you need a place to stay, right?"

I try to swallow the sticky lump lodged in the back of my throat. "Yeah, I'm... I don't want to go back there. At least, not any time soon."

"Then it's settled. You'll stay with me."

"I don't want to put you out."

"Oh, shut up," my big brother says with a chuckle. "What's family for?"

I manage a small smile. There may be a ten-year difference between us, but William's always been a protective and loving brother. Our schedules were the definition of chaotic when I went to college and he was still serving with the Marines, but we always made the time to call each other when we were able. In many ways, I think of William as my best friend and guardian angel.

"You're sure you're not too busy with work?" I ask, giving his suit a sideways glance. "I know you've been trying to get your startup off the ground."

William shrugs. "I'll admit I have an important meeting to get to in Seattle. I'll be away for about a month, but that doesn't change the fact that you need a place to stay."

I grimace. "You were on your way to the airport when I called, weren't you?"

"Maybe."

"I'm so sor—"

"Stop it, Winona. It's fine. My personal assistant can book me a flight for tomorrow. Or I can just cancel my whole trip and—"

"No," I say quickly. "No, please don't do that on my account. I'll be fine as long as I have a place to crash. You don't have to worry about leaving me alone."

William sits up a little straighter, his mouth dropping open. "Oh, shit."

"What?"

"Actually, you wouldn't be alone. A couple of my friends are staying at my place right now. You remember the guys from my old unit, don't you? Asher, Tank, Eddie, and Richard?"

I search my memories. My brain's admittedly a little jumbled right now, still buzzing on adrenaline. When my brother was an active service member, I got to meet some of the people he served with, though it was a very long time ago and I honestly haven't given them much thought.

"Vaguely," I answer.

William runs a hand through his hair, looking rather guilty. "It totally slipped my mind. They just got back from overseas and needed a place to relax for a while. They said they'll be leaving the weekend after the Fourth of July, but if you're uncomfortable with the idea, I can put you up in a hotel instead."

The thought of my brother paying for a room leaves a bitter taste in my mouth. He missed his flight to come and get me, rushing to my aid at the drop of a hat. It wouldn't feel right to ask him to pay for a room when I know for a fact he's got several unused guest rooms at his place.

"It's okay," I insist. "I don't mind at all. You trust these guys, right?"

"With my life."

"Then I trust them, too. Really, William, it's fine. I'm just grateful you came all this way for me."

"Are you kidding? I'd murder that son of a bitch with my own two hands if you asked me to."

I laugh quietly, but the dark look in my brother's eyes tells me he's probably not joking. "I'll have to figure out how to get the rest of my things from him."

"We'll worry about that later," he insists. "For now, let's get you home so you can rest. Are you sure you don't want to file a police report?"

I swallow hard, my throat uncomfortably dry. This is the third time he's asked me, but my answer remains the same. I might be scared and pissed off and unbelievably hurt, but a part of me just wants to move on.

"I just want to get out of here," I confess.

"Fair enough. Come on, my car's over there."

The drive to our parents' old lake house is as scenic and beautiful as I remember. The property is roughly a half-hour drive north of Sandy Creek, New York, surrounded on all sides by tall pines and a west-facing view of the water. Mom and Dad left it to both of us in their will, but I gave my half of the deed to William because Chet said he'd buy us a place of our own. What a fool I was.

By the time we arrive, the sky is an inky black. The stars are out and twinkling, but it's hard for me to enjoy the view—mostly because I'm not in the mood, but also because my left eye is officially so swollen I can barely see out of it. I haven't used the car visor's mirror at all during the drive because I'm a little worried about what I'll see. Judging by the pitying glances my brother's been giving me, I'd say not so good.

When the crunch of the gravel driveway beneath the car tires reaches my ear, I finally look out the window. Three other vehicles and a cool sporty motorcycle that definitely doesn't strike me as William's style are parked out front. Some of the lights are on inside, a warm and welcoming orange glow.

William tries to carry my heavy duffle bag in, but I won't let him. Instead, he grabs the door for me as we ascend the steps of the lake house's wraparound porch. The porch swing I used to use every day as a little girl is still there near the door, but its hinges are rusted, and the wood needs a fresh coat of paint. Memories of a simpler time bring a smile to my face— which unfortunately isn't very wide because everything hurts right about now.

My brother and I step inside together, the sounds of lighthearted chatter bouncing off the smooth walls and high ceiling. Men's voices, low and rumbling like distant thunder. It sounds like they're in the kitchen.

"Come on," William says. "I called ahead to let them know you were coming."

I'm not entirely sure who or what I was expecting to find when I follow William into the kitchen, but four hulking, handsome, irresistible men is definitely not it. Their conversation comes to an abrupt stop when they see me, a sudden awkwardness lingering in the air.

Damn, I must really look frightful.

"Boys, you remember my little sister, don't you?" William asks. He turns to me and gestures to the man furthest to the left, seated at the table in what used to be Dad's chair. "Winona, this is Asher Grey."

He stands and offers his hand to shake, a charming smile on his lips. His long fingers easily wrap around my own, the warmth of his palm igniting something deep inside me. Asher is breathtaking. Tall and broad, with dark brown hair and equally dark brown eyes that remind me of toiled earth after a heavy thunderstorm.

"Hi," he says, sounding almost... stunned? Caught off guard? I suppose I can't blame him. I'd be at a loss for words if some random woman showed up out of the blue with one hell of a shiner.

I shake his hand and offer a sheepish smile. "Hello."

My brother moves on to the next man, who immediately gets out of his seat. "That's Joseph Quill. We just call him Tank."

"Ma'am," he says as he nods respectfully. The first thing I notice about him is his unmistakable southern twang. His accent, combined with the low, full tone of his voice sends a delightful shiver down my spine.

It's frankly no wonder they call him Tank. He's certainly built like one. Strong arms, a wide chest, and thick neck make him a dominating presence. His dirty blonde hair is cropped short, his blue eyes trained on me like a hawk. It's hard for me to notice the sling around his right arm, propping it up against his chest.

My brother moves on. "The grumpy guy in all black is Edward Luna."

The third man in question glares daggers at William from his spot at the kitchen counter. "Watch it, Wren," he grumbles before tipping his chin up in my direction in greeting. "S'up?"

I can see why William thinks the guy's grumpy. He stands out in his all-black ensemble—black jeans, black sweatshirt, black hair—and I'm not sure if he's ever cracked a smile. His features are hard and cold, from the razor-sharp line of his jaw to his aquiline nose to his black irises like polished obsidian.

"Don't mind Eddie," the last man says to me with a low chuckle. "He's just cranky because his blood sugar is low." He rises from his chair and approaches, something mesmerizing in the way he moves. Slow, but powerful—a panther on the prowl.

The more I stare at his face, the more I start to recognize him. Streaks of grey pepper his dark brown hair, just like his trimmed beard. His eyes are a hypnotic green, much like the rich pines just outside. His name is on the tip of my tongue, but it takes me a moment to find it.

"Richard Wilder," I say with a gentle smile.

"You remember me?"

"You were there the day William was supposed to ship out on his first tour. I couldn't have been older than eight, nine?"

Beside me, my brother laughs. "Oh, right! You started bawling your eyes out and wouldn't let go of me. Richard had to pry you off."

Heat pools in my cheeks, mild embarrassment washing over me. "Sorry about that."

Richard carefully reaches for my hand and brings it up to his lips, placing a kiss on my knuckles. It's a gentlemanly, chaste sort of kiss, but it nonetheless sends electricity zapping up my spine. "There's nothing to apologize for."

Asher, Tank, Eddie, and Richard continue to stare at me, but their initial shock is nowhere to be found. If anything, it's been replaced with intrigue.

"Would you like something to eat?" Tank offers. I really like the way he talks. "We've got a lasagna in the fridge we could pop in the microwave for you."

"That's really sweet of you, but I think I want to lie down. It's, um, been a long day."

Asher nods. "If there's anything you need, just let us know."

I look at each in turn. My nerves are frayed and I'm not in a good headspace, so you'd think having a bunch of strangers in my childhood home would make me even more flighty. But I'm oddly at peace here. Maybe it's because I know William would never invite questionable characters to stay over, or perhaps it's the comfort of being in a familiar place that sets my mind at ease.

Or maybe it's because of the way the four of them are looking at me...

I can sense their outrage on my behalf. They're too polite to pry, but it goes without saying what's happened. I see a subtle shift in their posture, something leaning toward an innate protectiveness. I can see the questions written all over their faces and in their body language. It's in the tension of Asher's shoulders, the concern in Tank's eyes, the flex and clench of Eddie's hand, and the tick of Richard's jaw. Much like my brother, they look murderous and ready to fight Chet in an instant even though they don't even know who he is—all for my honor.

Of course, it could be my imagination. I *did* get hit pretty hard, after all. There's a good chance my brain is just desperate for a knight in shining armor since my Prince Charming turned out to be an absolute dick.

"Thank you," I mumble.

William pats me on the shoulder. "Get some rest, Winona. We can talk more in the morning."

I nod wearily and start down the hall, eager for this awful day to end.

CHAPTER 2

ASHER

I have a new assignment for you.
When are you coming back to work?

I stare at my grandfather's text message until the letters are burned into the back of my eye sockets. He sent the message almost a week ago, but I've left him on read. It doesn't feel good, but neither does having him breathing down my neck 24/7.

After how everything went down in Somalia, I think the boys and I are more than a little entitled to a well-deserved break. Tank's still recovering, for fuck's sake. Not to mention Eddie's still dealing with the trauma. He's too much of a tough guy to say it aloud, but these walls are thin. I've heard him screaming in the middle of the night, his nightmares clawing mercilessly through his psyche. And Richard... he and I aren't really talking to each other right now. Until he's done trying to play the blame game, I don't want anything to do with him.

The colonel knows there's next to nothing I wouldn't do for him, but we're not machines. We need rest just as much as anyone else.

I hear someone shuffling around in the kitchen, the soft clink and clatter of pots and pans floating into my ear. The time on my phone's screen reads 5:45 a.m. The boys and I are all early risers, but not *this* early. And certainly not while off-duty. Curious, I throw off my covers and quietly leave my room, padding down the hall.

I'm pleasantly surprised by the smell of sizzling bacon, freshly brewed coffee, and something coated heavily in cinnamon. A woman's soothing voice hums melodiously—the voice of an angel.

I round the corner slowly, silently, thoroughly breathless when I see Winona in front of the stove expertly flipping a pancake with nothing more than momentum and her hand on the pan handle.

From behind, it's hard not to notice the lovely curve of her ass, the dip of her slender waist, and her enticingly long legs. She's in a pair of light blue jogging shorts and a white tank top, exposing the smooth paleness of her skin.

My parents always taught me it was impolite to stare, but no matter what I do, I can't seem to look away, suddenly gripped by something carnal and feverish. Is it the delicate flow of her movements as she cooks? Or maybe it's the way her long, brunette hair flows over her shoulders, curled slightly at the ends from sleep? Or could it be the way she dips forward slightly, her shirt riding up just so to expose the small of her back?

And then she turns, and I'm suddenly reminded of the bastard who raised a hand to her. I don't know shit about the guy, but I hate him with all my being. How he could ever harm such a woman is beyond me. If the only way to get his point across is to use his fists, then he's not a fucking man at all.

William wouldn't tell us exactly what happened, only that he canceled his flight to Seattle last minute because there was some sort of family emergency. His text messages are always brief, sometimes impossible to decipher. Then Winona arrived late last night, shivering not from the cold, but from fear and exhaustion. It was easy to put two and two together.

Winona lets out a breathy yelp when she finally notices me. "Oh! H-how long were you standing there?"

"Only a moment," I lie. I smile at the smorgasbord she's single-handedly prepared, several plates piled high with food hot and ready on the kitchen table. "You must have quite the appetite," I joke lightly.

Miracle of miracles, I earn a little laugh from her. "I couldn't really sleep," she confesses, wringing her hands together. "I thought maybe you guys would like breakfast. Hungry?"

"Famished."

"Please, help yourself. Would you like some coffee?"

"I can get it. Why don't you sit down and enjoy?"

Winona nods, smiling appreciatively. We move at the same time. She crosses to the table while I attempt to get to the coffee maker. Unfortunately, the kitchen is rather small. More of a nook. Our paths cross, collide, and suddenly we're doing that awkward shuffle-dance to try and get out of each other's way.

"Sorry," she says with a light laugh, attempting to side-step me.

"No, it's okay—" I step to the side, too, but I'm too big for her to get around.

"I'll just go—"

"Here," I say with a chuckle, grasping her by the waist. I lift her up and rotate our positions, setting her down on the tile floor. My eyes didn't deceive me—she's as wonderfully soft as she looks.

But I realize my mistake all too late. Her laughter fades, her eyes cast to the floor. Winona clears her throat, shifting her weight uncomfortably as her cheeks redden. I've made her uneasy. I couldn't help myself, but that was no excuse. What the hell was I thinking? Touching her without her permission only hours after someone close to her did the same? As innocent as my intentions were, it was still wrong of me.

"Sorry about that," I mutter.

When Winona looks at me, I don't see discomfort or fear. If anything, her eyes are ablaze, so bewitching it makes my heart skip a beat. "It's alright," she says calmly, the corners of her lips tugging up into a grin.

I reflect her smile, amused and a little dazed. *Holy shit, William's little sister is gorgeous*—black eye aside, and even then, it's not that bad. The swelling has gone down slightly, but the bruise is more apparent than it was last night. Reddish purples and pinks. All things considered, the injury isn't too bad. It doesn't look like she's hurt anywhere else, and for some reason, I'm immensely grateful for that fact.

"Let me get you an ice pack," I mumble, barely audible in my own ears.

I turn quickly and head straight to the refrigerator, opening the top door to the freezer. William's got a couple of those reusable ice packs shoved way in the back, so I grab one and wrap it up with the nearest clean tea towel I can find. Slowly, I place it on her eye. Her hand follows, her fingers gingerly grazing my wrist before settling on the back of my hand, keeping me there.

I'm suddenly incendiary, my skin feverishly hot beneath her touch. I'm up close; I can pick up the lovely scent of her sweet floral perfume—roses and peaches. My gaze slips down to the plush full-ness of her mouth, and I'm lost in the shape of her sharp cupid's bow and soft bottom lip.

My mouth goes dry and my heart hammers against my ribcage. Why do I want to devour her lips? Why do I want to press her against the edge of the counter and see if the rest of her body is as hot and welcoming as it looks? These are *not* thoughts I should be having about one of my closest friend's little sister, and yet...

Why is she looking at me like that? Does she feel this strange pull between us, too? Could she possibly—

"Oh, sweet! Pancakes!"

Winona and I jolt, each taking a massive step apart just as William and Eddie enter. Neither of them seem the wiser, too fixated on breakfast to notice Winona's pink cheeks and my semi-hard cock hidden by my shorts. Fuck, what's gotten into me this morning?

"Are Tank and Richard still asleep?" I ask, making my way over to the counter as casually as possible. I take my time making my coffee, hoping my body will calm down.

"You know them," William says lightly, helping himself to several strips of bacon. "They could sleep through a hurricane."

"Did you sleep okay?" Winona asks when she takes her seat next to Eddie. "I, uh... I thought I heard you yelling last night."

I say nothing, taking a long sip of my coffee. Black with one sugar. I've tried to bring the issue up with Eddie countless times since we got back, but he always ends up chewing my ear off. I'm not trying to antagonize him. The four of us went through hell and back, and a weaker soldier would have lost his mind after what we witnessed. All I want is for Eddie to get help—but he has to admit there's a problem, first.

I half expect him to cuss Winona out. He may be a Marine, but he's got the mouth of a fucking sailor. Maybe I should step in and change the subject before—

"I slept fine," he grumbles around a mouthful of cheesy scrambled eggs.

Huh. Color me surprised.

"I'm glad," she says, and I think she genuinely means it.

"What about you?" he asks gruffly. Everything out of his mouth sounds like a damn machine gun, sharp and to the point and with much too much force. Luckily, Winona doesn't seem to think much of it.

She shrugs. "Good. Alright."

William strums his fingers on the table's surface. "Has he tried contacting you?"

His sister presses her lips into a thin line. "Yes. He blew up my phone all night and all morning. I texted him that I'm fine and not to contact me, but he won't stop, so I turned off my phone."

"I don't have to go on this trip, Win."

She shoots him an exasperated look. "We've been over this. I'll be okay here, I swear."

My ears perk up. "Is this the boyfriend?"

"*Ex*," she corrected pointedly. "But yes."

"I know it's probably none of our business, but does he know about this place?"

Winona chews on the inside of her cheek. "I never told him about my parents' lake house. He shouldn't be able to find me here."

"How long is she staying?" Eddie asks William.

"As long as she needs."

Eddie huffs and looks at her. "Let's not beat around the bush, okay? Is this asshole going to try and track you down? We need to know these things." His expression is hard and impassable. "What about your job? Do you need to tell your boss you'll need time off? Did you leave anything important behind? Does he know how to locate you using your phone?"

I sigh. "Don't overwhelm her, man."

Winona sits up a little straighter, unperturbed. She answers without missing a beat. "I'm a freelance editor, so I'm my own boss. I did leave a couple of keepsakes at his place, but I'll figure out how to get them back at a later date. And no, he doesn't know how. Even if he did, my phone is off, so there'd be no signal to pinpoint me."

William cackles. I stifle a laugh. Eddie just shrugs and attacks his piece of buttered toast like it owes him money.

"I think that's settled, then," William says. "I think there's a flight this afternoon I can catch, but if you need anything at all, you'd better call me."

Winona smiles. "I will."

CHAPTER 3

TANK

Winona hugs her brother tight, hopping up on the tips of her toes in order to reach. They're by his car, too far away for any of us to overhear their conversation. They speak quietly, a couple of nods here and there followed by reassuring smiles.

With one final wave to the boys, William gets in his car and backs out of the gravel driveway, disappearing around the bend not long after. There's no need for personalized goodbyes because he already pulled the four of us aside to give one final warning before his trip.

Protect my sister at all costs.

And if any of you make a move on her, I'll personally castrate you.

Needless to say, we got his message loud and clear. Except...

I don't know about Asher, Eddie, and Richard, but I have a feeling keeping my word to William is going to be easier said than done. Winona is doggone gorgeous. Ever since I first laid eyes on her, I've been as happy as a clam at high tide. They should bottle up whatever her sweet smiles are made of, because I swear it's more effective than the pain meds the doctors have me on.

We got back from overseas roughly two weeks ago, and I've been swimming in pain like nothing I've ever experienced. I still don't know what went wrong. None of us do. But the fact of the matter is we're lucky to be alive. The surgeons said they had one hell of a time getting the shrapnel out of my arm, but with some time and patience, I'll be patched up good as new.

I have plenty of time since we're on leave...But I don't have the patience. Not even a lick.

Winona turns and walks up to the porch, her hand gliding up the support rail. "He told me to tell you all to be good."

I chuckle good-naturedly. "Yeah, that's about right."

"Do you have any plans for the day?" she asks, blinking up at us with those pretty hazel eyes. The curl of her long lashes and the shape of her little button nose does something strange to my insides. I can't remember the last time I had a case of butterflies as bad as this one.

"We're on vacation," Asher offers with a charming smile. "We've got nowhere important to be. Why do you ask?"

She tucks a few loose strands of her hair behind her ear. "Well, I guess I didn't pack as well as I thought last night, so I need to head into town to buy a few things. Since I don't have a car, I was wondering if one of you would be willing to—"

"I'll take you," Eddie says, which is frankly a surprise and a half. I love the man like a brother, but he's never been the type to willingly lend a hand—especially when there's nothing to be gained. But the way he looks at her tells me everything I need to know. Maybe I'm not the only one who's going to have a hard time keeping our promise to William.

"Hop on the back of my bike," Eddie continues.

"Why don't we *all* go into town," I suggest. "No harm in a change of scenery, right?"

Asher and Richard exchange a heated glare. The silence between them speaks volumes. Apparently, they're still at it. Things have been particularly stressful since we failed our mission, and neither knows where to pin the blame for the catastrophic shitshow that went down. I'm really hoping it all blows over soon. I can't stand seeing my brothers at odds with one another.

Winona notices the exchange but says nothing about it. "I think that's wonderful. It's been a long time since I've visited town. I'd love to see what's changed."

"We'll take my car," Richard says before anyone else can offer.

People stare wherever we go, whispering amongst themselves as Winona passes them by. I'm not sure if she's aware of all the strange looks or if she's choosing to ignore them. Either way, she doesn't appear to be bothered as she flits from storefront to storefront, merrily browsing.

"So, where are you from again?" she asks me as we stroll. "I feel like you might have told me ages ago at a Birthday Ball, but I can't remember."

"Alabama, ma'am. Born and raised."

Winona snaps her fingers. "Oh, that's right! A little ways outside of Florence."

I grin proudly, genuinely surprised she bothered to remember the conversation at all. She couldn't have been older than thirteen or fourteen. Vivid memories of her frilly pink dress dance through my mind. I hadn't paid much attention to her back then. She was glued to her brother's hip all night, anyway, and there were plenty of pretty ladies in need of a dance partner. But now?

Now, I can't *stop* paying attention to her.

The delicious plane of her throat, perfect for kissing. Her ample bosom and her small waist, perfect for holding. Her luscious, long locks—perfect for pulling.

I mentally berate myself. This is wrong. It hasn't even been two hours since William left, and my mind's already getting away from me. I can't be thinking these things—these delicious, dirty things—for three very important reasons: she's much too young, at least ten years between us; there's no doubt in my mind William *will* make good on his threat to castrate me; and she's clearly going through a bad breakup under very traumatic circumstances. I'm sure she doesn't want to exchange one asshole for another.

"Asher tells me you're a freelance editor," I say as she peers into a dress shop. "Books and stuff. Mighty impressive."

"He told you?" she says coyly. "Goodness, word gets around fast at the lake house."

I chuckle. "We tell each other everything. We're worse than my Nana's knitting circle after a pitcher of margaritas."

Winona laughs. *Really* laughs. The sound is bright and bubbly, so beautiful it takes my breath away. It's warmer than sunshine and more refreshing than an April shower. "That's quite an image."

"It's the truth. Once Nana knocks a few back, she'll spout everyone's secrets no problem."

"She sounds like a lot of fun."

"Oh, she's the best."

"Do you get to see her often?"

"Not so much anymore," I confess. "But that's okay. My sisters keep her plenty entertained while I'm abroad."

Her smile widens. "Sisters?"

"Seven, in fact."

"You're kidding. Are you older? Somewhere in the middle?"

"I'm the youngest, actually. They babied me all the time. Still do, matter of fact. I can't go a week without them calling to check up on me."

Winona giggles. "I guess we have that in common, huh? What about—Wait a second."

"What is it?"

"Where are the others?"

I stop in my tracks and turn, realizing Asher, Eddie, and Richard are no longer with us. I have a sneaking suspicion why they might have ventured off on their own, but I'd rather not worry Winona.

"Something shiny probably caught Eddie's eye," I joke lightly.

"I'm sure they'll catch up with us soon. Is there anywhere else you'd like to go while we're in town?"

She casts a curious glance over my shoulder, but says, "Maybe this dress shop? I accidentally packed all my winter sweaters, so I'm hoping to find something light for the weather."

I hold the door open for her with a grand sweep of my hand. "After you, ma'am."

The shop is cramped, but that's true for most places when you're my size. Clothing racks are arranged in tight rows, and the width of my body takes up the entire aisle. But as I watch Winona browse through the clothes and pick out a few summer dresses, my discomfort slowly dissipates. I notice little things, like how she prefers simple patterns in bright colors, or when she glances at the price and deems it too expensive, her nose curls adorably before she puts the item back on the rack.

"What's wrong with that one?" I ask her.

Winona huffs. "It costs a hundred and twenty bucks."

"Didn't William say you could put everything on his card?"

"Yes, but I'd feel guilty buying something that expensive on his dime. There's nothing wrong with a fifteen-dollar dress."

I decide I don't want to hear any of it. I pluck the dress off the rack and hand it to her. "Go try it on."

"It's too expensive, Tank."

"No harm in taking it for a test drive, though, right?"

Winona takes the dress, laughing under her breath. "Why do I have a feeling you won't take no for an answer?"

"Because I won't. I think you can get changed over there."

There are a couple of stalls in the back corner of the boutique shop, nothing but a flimsy navy curtain for privacy. I guess this place isn't big enough for a private change room.

"Will you stand watch?" Winona asks, her voice as sweet as honey.

I chuckle. "Don't worry, I'll protect you from any looky-loos."

She steps into the stall while I remain just on the other side of the curtain, observing the other shoppers and noting the exits. I know I'm not on duty right now, but old habits die hard. The throb of my healing arm serves as a reminder to always be on guard. My injury is proof that things can go wrong at the turn of a dime, and while I don't expect any trouble in this quaint little town, I'd rather play it safe than sorry.

I take a quick glance out the store's street-facing windows and spot the boys on the other side of the street next to the public water feature. I obviously have no idea what they're saying, but their body language speaks volumes. I think Asher and Richard are finally getting at it, and poor Eddie is caught in the middle of it. I really hope those two can work things out—and sooner rather than later.

"Tank?" Winona calls out softly. I hear the curtain pulling aside.

"Yeah, sugar?" I don't even mean to use the endearment, it just sort of slips out. It's fitting, I think, since everything about her is so sweet it's enough to make my teeth hurt. Thankfully, Winona doesn't seem to take issue.

"Would you mind helping me with the zipper?" she asks. "I can't quite reach."

Before I can answer, Winona turns and exposes the soft, milky surface of her back. I have no sweet clue why my hand is so shaky. I've been trapped under enemy fire. Nearly blown up by an IED. Tasked with leading full-on assault raids in the dead of night, enemies surrounding us on all sides—but *this* makes me nervous?

Slowly, carefully, I drag the zipper of her dress up, intently following the line of her spine. My knuckles graze her bare skin. There's something electric in the air. It makes the hairs on my arms stand on end, the space between us thick and heavy with anticipation. I almost hate that the zipper isn't longer, because before I know it, the job's done and I know I can't stay.

When I look up, I find Winona watching me in the reflection of the changing stall's mirror. Her eyes darken with something intense and hungry, but I'm no better. My own expression is full of obvious want and a burning focus. I guess I don't have as good of a poker face as I thought.

Could it be how irresistible she looks in that dress? Or maybe it's the fact that she's off limits that has me in a tailspin. Or is it because she reminds me so much of an abandoned kitten in need of safe keeping?

I could protect her, if she wanted. I could keep her safe.

"Maybe I'll get the dress, after all," she mumbles.

We're still staring at each other, but it isn't awkward. It's charged and tense, neither of us willing to be the first to break. Except I do because what other choice do I have?

"We should get going," I mumble. "I think the guys are waiting outside."

"Okay. Let me just change and I'll—"

"Wear it out. It looks good on you."

Her cheeks flush pink. "I still have to pay for it."

My fingers graze the nape of her delicate neck and slip just beneath the collar of the dress. I find the price tag and quickly swipe it off her. "I'll take care of it," I said. "Consider it a homecoming present."

Winona gives me an appreciative smile, a protest on her lips, so I turn on my heels and walk straight to the cashier. I'm happy to do it. There's frankly nothing nicer than treating the little lady to something she more than deserves.

And I think a fine belle like Winona deserves it all.

CHAPTER 4

EDDIE

Here they fucking go.

I was starting to wonder when this weird, pent-up anger between Asher and Richard would finally blow up in our faces. I had half a mind to start taking bets. They've been tense ever since we got back from our botched mission, and it's no secret they blame each other for how everything went down.

Asher likes to call this a vacation, but we all know the truth. It's a mandated sabbatical while the higher-ups investigate what the hell went wrong.

"I'm telling you someone sold us out!" Richard exclaims, a sort of shout-whisper so as to not draw the attention of civilians passing by.

Asher folds his arms over his chest, his lips pressed into a thin line. "Why can't you accept it was an accident? Shit happens."

"*Shit happens?*" Richard echoes, practically seething. "We lost three good men that day. Tank almost had his arm blown off! And Eddie—"

"Don't drag me into this," I snap.

My brothers give me a look that says *you're kidding, right?* I hate it so fucking much. Since we got back, Asher's been trying to force feed the idea of going to therapy down my throat, and Richard's been pulling me aside frequently to "check on things." But I tell them the same thing every single time.

I'm fine. Nothing's wrong with me. I walked away unscathed.

Save for the nightmares. And the fact that I can't stop seeing the carnage, the bodies of our fallen comrades. The blood, the screaming and confusion. Sometimes I wake up in the middle of the night in a cold sweat, only to realize I'm still trapped in the middle of one of my dreams. I can still hear the gunfire, the explosions. The smell of iron fills my nose and coats my tongue. There's nowhere to retreat. Nowhere to run.

But I'm fine.

Totally fine.

"Then let's hear it," Asher grumbles. "Who do you want to pin the blame on now?"

Richard sets his jaw, cold fury in his eyes. "Colonel George Grey."

His answer surprises me. Asher, too, judging by the way his face pales.

"You think his grandfather set us up?" I ask harshly. "Dude, you're way off base here."

"Am I?" he challenges. "It was an off the books op. Only a handful of people knew what was going on, the details on a need-to-know basis. Jameson, Reiko, and Fischer clearly weren't in on it, otherwise their wives wouldn't have buried them last week. And I *know* none of us would betray each other. Leaves only one logical answer."

Asher shakes his head furiously, the vein at his temple pulsing. "No. No fucking way. He'd never do that to us."

"You're just saying that because you're biased."

"I'm saying it because he has no reason to turn on us!" Asher roars at the top of his lungs. He lowers his voice as he continues. "Familial relation aside, let's say I consider it and take you at your word. Do you even have any evidence?"

Richard doesn't say anything, just flares his nostrils and grits his teeth. It's answer enough.

"Look," Asher says. "That night... What happened was unthinkable. We were unprepared, and we suffered the consequences. But pointing fingers isn't going to make the situation better. I know you feel responsible because you were leading the charge, but what's done is done. We can't change the past. All we can do is rest, recover, and move on."

I scoff. Move on? I've known Asher and Richard for a very long time. We've been through thick and thin together, so I know them better than most. In many ways, they're opposites. Asher has always been the good Marine, the yes man, a shining example everyone should strive to emulate. Richard's always been gruff, downright guerilla, and never takes shit lying down. But they do have one thing in common—they're both stubborn as fuck and they make it everyone else's problem.

"Enough," I snap, irritation crawling through my muscles. "Wrap this up so we can get the fuck out of here." There's a pounding pressure behind my eyes, probably from lack of sleep. We've been away from Winona too long, and it's starting to make me a little antsy.

She has me feeling some type of way, because whenever I get within three feet of her, my chest suddenly tightens and my palms get clammy. I don't like it. Everything about her has me teetering on the edge, like I don't know whether I'm coming or going. She's a walking warning sign. She's trouble wrapped up in a nice five-foot-fuck-all package.

She makes me nervous, and I don't know why. I want to stare at her pretty face, but I don't want to creep her out. I want to talk to her, but I'm more than aware that I'm the furthest thing from Shakespeare. I don't have Asher's kindness, Tank's charm, or Richard's surety.

I'm rough and mean and all I do is break things—and the last thing I want is to break her.

"I don't have any evidence yet," Richard says. "But I will. I won't stop looking. I'm not willing to chalk everything up to being an accident. We were *ambushed*. Nobody should have known we were coming."

Asher sighs, his anger coming off him in waves. "Don't do this, man. You're making a mistake."

"I'm starting to think you're protecting the old man."

"Yes, from unfounded claims."

"Mark my words, I will get to the bottom of this—"

"Um, guys?"

The pleasant sound of a woman's voice interrupts us. The three of us turn to find Winona standing close, a couple of shopping bags in her hands. She's dressed differently, having purchased a pretty periwinkle summer dress that brings out the sparkling color of her eyes. She looks like she should be prancing in a field somewhere making flower crowns. She's so fucking beautiful to look at it almost hurts my eyes.

"All done?" Asher asks, easily slipping into his cheery persona with a big smile.

Richard, too, drops their argument like it never happened, turning all his attention towards her. "You look lovely."

"Thank you. Tank bought it for me."

I arch a brow and shoot him a pointed glare. "Let's get something to eat before we head back," I say. "I don't feel like cooking lunch for your sorry asses."

Winona glances at me wryly. "You cook?"

Tank swings his good arm over my shoulder with a hearty laugh. "This guy right here is the best damn cook in the whole Marine Corps!"

"Who doesn't feel like cooking tonight, so pick somewhere."

"Chinese," Asher and Richard both say at the exact same time. They briefly glare at each other before breaking eye contact like petulant children.

"I have a hankering for fajitas, actually," Tank comments.

I ignore the three of them. There's really only one person I want to hear from. I hold Winona's flighty gaze and ask, "What about you?"

She glances between the four of us before sheepishly wringing her fingers together. "I'm kind of craving a burger and some fries. Maybe a vanilla milkshake? It's been a while since I've had one."

I've personally never been a fan of sweet things or greasy spoon establishments, but I really want to see Winona smile. It feels like a reward, a tiny hit of dopamine that keeps me on the tips of my toes, eager for the next.

My answer goes without saying, but that doesn't stop me from glancing at the boys. "Anyone got a problem with burgers and fries?"

The response is a resounding no.

The five of us are crammed together in a booth near the back of the diner, a local mom and pop joint that doesn't skimp on the fries and has unlimited soda refills. The food's delicious and blessedly cheap. Color me impressed.

Winona sits between Tank and me, while Asher and Richard look like they're two seconds away from killing each other on the other side of the booth. I think Winona's starting to catch on, but she's too polite to say anything about it to their faces. I love my brothers to death, but sometimes they can be real fucking crybabies.

Once she's finished her plate, Winona leans back and lets out a satisfied moan, patting her belly with a happy smile. "That hit the spot."

Sitting beside her might have been a mistake. She smells too good, and I like the feeling of her knee occasionally bumping against mine way too much. Plus, because of our height difference, I may or may not have managed to sneak a peek down the low cut of her dress. I don't know if that was intentional on Tank's part, but I have to resist the urge to give him a high five.

"So, what do you guys do in your free time?" she asks sweetly.

"William used to always complain about how bored he was when he had time off between tours. Civilian life isn't very action-packed, apparently."

I think back to the days when William was still a part of our little crew. He left the Marines a couple of years ago to pursue starting a company of his own. He's always been an ideas kind of man, so it was no surprise he'd eventually branch off and do his own thing. I do miss him, though. He's got the level head, killer aim, and a can-do attitude I'm sorely lacking. In many ways, we balanced each other out.

"I used to raise chickens," Tank says. What a typical thing for him to say. But while I roll my eyes, Winona's face lights up.

"Really?"

"My sisters had all manner of rabbits and baby goats to look after on the family farm. I eventually got around to building them a hutch. One thing led to another, and I had a coop all built up for chickens and ducks and geese. Nana's looking after them for me right now. I'm hoping to make a pitstop down South after the Fourth of July weekend. After that, we have to ship off again."

Winona's brows furrow. "So soon... But what about your arm?"

Across the table, Asher laughs. "Don't worry. He's tough. He'll be right as rain in no time."

"Do you already know where you're being sent? Or is that, like, confidential?"

"It's *supposed* to be," Richard grumbles. "But no, we don't know yet. We just know we have to get back to base after the long weekend."

Asher's phone rings in his pocket, interrupting our conversation. He answers quickly. I'm not in a position to see his screen, but one look at Richard's darkened expression is the only hint I need.

"Hey, Gramps," Asher answers. He mutters a quick *excuse me* before slipping out of the booth to take the call.

"I'll go pay and bring the car around," Richard says hastily.

Winona sits up a bit straighter. "Oh, no, please let me."

Richard waves her off with a gentle smile. It's the calmest I've seen him in quite a while. "Don't worry about it, Win. It's our treat."

"You guys better be careful. I'm starting to feel spoiled."

Tank chuckles good-naturedly. "Better get used to it. William made us promise to take good care of you." He slides out of the booth, too. "Gonna pop by the restroom real quick."

And then there were two.

Winona doesn't move away despite the extra leg room. She's still pressed against me, our thighs and the sides of our arms touching. As she delicately reaches for the last of her milkshake, she blinks up at me. "Want some?"

"I don't like sweets," I answer gruffly. Too gruffly. What the fuck is wrong with my volume control? Maybe all my years with the Marines have trained it out of me. I'm either shouting orders or shouting my reply.

Winona doesn't seem the least bit perturbed. She turns slightly in her seat, holding the rim of her tall milkshake glass in front of me. "It's *really* good. Here, let me grab you a clean straw—"

I dip down and wrap my lips around her straw, taking a few deep gulps. Her eyes flick down to my mouth. I see no disgust or irritation, only dark intrigue. I'm personally not a fan of the beverage, the vanilla extract so overpowering it makes my jaw ache, but our indirect kiss makes it worth it.

She smiles coyly. "Well?"

"It's okay."

Winona brings the straw to her own lips and finishes the remaining remnants, never once breaking eye contact with me. Her flirting is subtle, but there's no denying she knows what she's doing to me. To *us*.

CHAPTER 5

RICHARD

I'm used to putting out fires. That's my job as the leader. When a problem arises, I'm there in an instant, trying to get to the bottom of things. And Winona is a problem.

A very distracting problem.

She hasn't escaped my notice. Far from it. From the moment I laid eyes on her, I haven't been able to look away. I'm floored at the beautiful woman she's become. It feels like just yesterday I was lifting her into a hug and offering her a firm reassurance that I'd keep her big brother safe on his very first tour overseas. Now she's all grown up, every bit elegant and graceful and stunning.

I can tell my men are all taken with her, too. I recognize the hunger in their eyes, the burning desire. Who can blame them? I certainly can't.

I'm not afraid of William or his threats. I've always been the kind of man who takes what he wants—and a pretty little bird like Winona is no exception—but the only reason I haven't made a move is because I still respect the man deeply. Before he left Winona in our charge, I gave him my word we'd look after her. Above all else, I am a man of honor.

No matter how badly I want to run my fingers through her hair. No matter how desperately I want to hear her soft moan in my ear. No matter how much I yearn to feel her thighs wrapped around me. My word is my bond. I cannot go back on it.

By the time we get back to the lake house, the sun is starting to set beyond the horizon, painting the skies in a wash of pinks, oranges, and soft yellows. The light catches the water of the lake, glimmering like starlight on its rippling surface. The breeze is warm and welcoming, bringing with it the scent of pines and rich earth from the surrounding properties. From what William told me, the families who live around here don't take up residence in their summer homes until mid-June when the weather is at its hottest, so for the next few weeks, we've got the lake all to ourselves.

"When do you want to get your stuff back from your ex?" Eddie asks bluntly. No easing into it, just straight to ripping off the Band-Aid. While I appreciate that he isn't the type to beat around the bush, I wish he'd handle Winona's situation a tad more delicately.

Winona sighs as we enter the main hall together. It's crowded as the five of us take off our coats and toe off our shoes by the door.

"I'd like to get it done as soon as possible," she says. "But I don't know what to expect. I haven't had my phone on this entire time. I'm scared he's going to be furious if I try calling to ask for my stuff back. Or he'll guilt trip me."

Tank snorts. "Buddy can fucking try."

"We're more than happy to go with you," Asher offers. Always such a good guy.

I've known him for a decade and he's almost incapable of seeing the bad in anyone—his conniving grandfather included, but I'm choosing not to focus on that right now. It'll only piss me off.

With a demure smile, Winona says, "Alright, let me go get my phone."

"We'll be here," Asher and I say at the exact same time. It sounds like a stereo.

Once Winona disappears down the hall, an awkward tension

blankets us. It's not usually this hard to be around them. There's next to nothing I wouldn't do for them. They've saved my life on several occasions, and I saved them all in return. After a handful of extremely close calls, the bond we've forged is stronger than steel.

They're more than just family to me, more than brothers, but I don't think there's a word in the English dictionary to describe just how close we are. There's really only one reason why things are so tense right now, but I don't see it resolving unless I give up my search for answers or Asher finally realizes I'm right—both outcomes are impossible.

"Stop yelling at me, Chet," Winona's voice carries from her room.

The wobble in her voice triggers something inside me. Inside all of us. All it takes is one look shared between me, Asher, Tank, and Eddie before we're rushing down the narrow hall of the lake house to get to her.

She hasn't even put the call on speaker, but we can hear her asshole ex-boyfriend loud and clear as he screams into her ear.

"I said I was sorry! Where the fuck are you, Winona? Come home right now!"

I fully expect Winona to start crying. The edges of her eyes are red and glossy, but she holds her ground, a steep frown knitting her brows together. She takes a deep breath, listening with far more patience than I could ever muster in a situation like this, and waits until Chet tires himself out.

"I'm breaking up with you, Chet," she says, clear and concise. "We're done."

"Babe, I told you it was an *accident*."

"You *wound up!*" Winona seethes.

"You're seriously going to flush four years down the toilet? I swear, I'll never do it again. You just wouldn't *shut up*."

"That's because you kept yelling over me."

"How many times am I going to have to apologize, Win? Don't you see that you're the one overreacting?"

"Don't try to gaslight me! You're the one who lost it when I told you about the internship."

"You should have told me about it sooner."

"I *tried*—"

"I was planning a vacation for us, Win. Somewhere in Italy. That's why I got so upset!"

Winona's left eye twitches. "You were planning a vacation in the *fall?*"

"Are you calling me a liar?"

"I didn't say that." She sighs heavily. "Look, there's nothing more to discuss here. We will be by tomorrow to pick up my things and to drop off my key."

"*We?*"

"This conversation is over." She hangs up and tosses her phone on her bed with a huff. "What a jerk."

The four of us hover by her doorway like eager puppies. I'm glad to know I'm not the only one so easily hypnotized by Winona's charm. There's just something about her that makes me want to wrap her in my arms and shield her from the world. But if that phone call was any indication, it's pretty clear the woman knows how to stand up for herself.

"Are you okay?" Tank asks her softly.

Winona quickly wipes her eyes dry before smiling at the four of us. I hate to see it. She doesn't need to pretend for our sake, but she does it anyway. "I apologize in advance for any trouble he gives you tomorrow."

Eddie laughs. "He'll be the sorry one."

The rest of the evening is blessedly uneventful. After Eddie whips up a light dinner of honey-lemon marinated salmon on a bed of fluffy white rice—I swear the man is the military version of Gordon Ramsay —I get ready to head out for a short walk before hitting the hay. I've been going on more and more walks recently, breathing in the fresh forest air. It's the only thing I can do to expel all the nervous energy.

I've always hated sitting still. There are too many thoughts in my head, too many ideas and questions rattling around inside my brain. The only time I feel remotely calm is when I'm working with my hands. I'm pretty sure that's why I took to Marine life so well. There's always another task, always another goal to achieve. The structure keeps me sane, keeps me too busy to be bogged down by my own mind.

While I'm grateful to William for letting us crash at his lake house, it's too damn quiet out here. Too serene and peaceful. I can't stay put long enough to enjoy the scenery or the sounds of the lake lapping at the sandy shore. I'm thankful for the hiking trails around these parts, because at least hiking feels a lot like marching.

I've barely made it past the porch swing before a soft voice reaches my ear.

"Where are you going?"

I turn to find Winona seated on the swing, gently rocking herself back and forth with the balls of her feet. Her beauty is a haunting one, illuminated by the soft silver light of the moon and the gentle orange glow of the singular porch light just above our heads. She's pulled her long brunette locks up into a messy bun, a steaming hot cup of tea in her hands.

"Just needed some fresh air," I reply. I know I wanted some time to myself, but I can't stand the thought of Winona all by her lonesome. Maybe she could use some company. "Would you like to join me?"

Winona doesn't hesitate, a sweet smile stretching across her lips. "I'd love to." She sets her tea aside and hops off the swing. I offer her my elbow, which she promptly slips her arm through.

Having her at my side is incredibly pleasant. Fallen leaves crunch underfoot and the early summer breeze rustles through the trees. Above us, the dark sky is littered with twinkling stars, their light reflecting delicately off the still surface of the lake. Our walk is aimless, our pace lazy and relaxed. If Winona is feeling nervous about tomorrow, she certainly does a good job of not showing it.

"It's really beautiful out here," she says, peering up at the sky.

"Did you know your brother and I once had to use the stars to navigate our way to base?"

"Really? I don't think he ever told me that story."

"Probably because he didn't want you to worry."

Winona laughs softly. "Checks out. So, what happened?"

"We were on a supply run, driving to and from base in the south of Iraq. Something was wrong with our Humvee's engine. Overheated. Wound up stranded out in the middle of the desert wasteland."

Winona's no longer looking at the stars, instead watching me with wide-eyed fascination. "Then what happened? Couldn't you just radio for help?"

"You'd think," I say with a smug grin. "But our luck went from bad to worse. We were caught in the middle of a sandstorm that messed with our equipment. We couldn't get a message back to base, so William and I decided to hunker down until the storm passed."

I've completely captured her attention. She holds onto my arm, practically pressing herself up against me as she waits for the grand finale.

"It was well after dark by the time the storm passed, and we'd been away for so long we were sure they'd send out a search party for us soon. It was imperative that we get back as soon as possible. Unfortunately, we were all turned around. William wanted to go in one direction, I wanted to go in another, but I taught him how to use the stars to gather our bearings. We hiked all the way back and made it before roll call the next morning."

The brilliant twinkle in her eyes could rival the stars above. "Teach me?"

I can't bring myself to tell her no. I step behind her and carefully place my hand below her wrist, guiding it upward to use her finger as a pointer. "That one there," I murmur against her ear. "That's the North Star."

"How can you tell?"

"Do you see how it's brighter than the rest?"

"Yes." Winona nods slightly, the scent of her hair filling my nose.

How did we end up this close? What is it about her that puts my thoughts on standby and quiets all the noise inside my head? At this exact moment, I realize I'm still holding her hand, her fingers grazing my own.

Now that I've locked on to the shape of her lips, I wonder how easy it would be to dip down and claim them. Would she let me? I wonder if she'd prefer it gentle and sweet, or rough and raw. Suddenly my head is no longer quiet, the voice in the back of my mind egging me on.

"Your hands are getting cold," she whispers, looking deep into my eyes.

"We should probably head back," I murmur, so lost in her orbit it's almost impossible for me to find the words.

I can't remember the last time a woman had this much sway over me. It's been ages since my last serious girlfriend, which was before I shipped off and dedicated my life to the Marines—almost twenty years ago. I don't understand why I'm so drawn to her, can't even begin to fathom the tightness in my chest when Winona's eyes flick down to my lips, too.

What is she waiting for? What am I waiting for?

"Come on," she says gently.

I don't complain when we start back together, her fingers threaded through mine like it's the most natural thing in the world.

CHAPTER 6

WINONA

I wake up the next morning in a tizzy.

After sending Chet a quick text explaining I'd be dropping
by around noon for my things, he proceeded to blow up my phone
with a series of apologies—all things he's repeated ad nauseam.

Babe, please let me make it up to you.
  What can I do to earn back your trust?
  I love you, Winona. Please don't do this.
  We can get through this together.
  Don't you love me?

The moment he tries to guilt trip me, I block his number. I really
don't need to be dealing with that right now. Chet and I have been
together since our first year of college. It started with a couple of shy
glances from across the classroom, then we were officially introduced
through a mutual friend, and the rest was history. We studied

together, pulled all-nighters together, got our first apartment together, graduated together. Chet and I were joined at the hip...

And maybe that's why I didn't see the red flags until I was hit square in the face by one.

My friends warned me about not getting swept up in the romance, not to wear my rose-colored glasses. But Chet was my first real boyfriend. In many ways, I thought we were perfect for each other. We have all the same interests, the same goals. He wants to be a published author one day, and I want to be an editor at a major publishing house. We were like two peas in a pod. Complimentary.

So, I ignored his sometimes-snide comments about my appearance, about the extra pounds I packed on during Christmas break. Sometimes people say hurtful things without thinking. It happens. He apologized profusely when I told him it upset me, and I forgave him almost ten minutes later.

I ignored his drinking. He worked part-time at a garage throughout college to make a little extra money. I remember being blown away by his work ethic, about how determined he was. If anyone deserves a cold beer at the end of a hard shift, it'd be Chet.

At the time, I didn't mind when one beer would turn into two, then three, and then he'd finish the whole six-pack before passing out in front of the TV. It was never really a problem because he always tidied up after himself in the morning, and it never affected his mood or how he treated me.

I think everything started to change after we graduated and moved into an apartment together. A *real* apartment, one in the heart of the city close to the new garage he worked at. While I got to stay home and work freelance jobs, Chet was out most of the day from nine to five, grinding away to earn his paycheck. He'd come home grumbling about how stupid customers were or how terribly his boss treated him—and I listened with a smile and doted on him, reminding him how much I appreciated how hard he worked.

Except he complained about *everything*. His long hours, how much his feet hurt at the end of the day, that our apartment was too small and he didn't make enough money. He complained about coming home so exhausted he could never find the time to write. And every single time, without fail, it was somehow *my* fault.

Why isn't dinner ready? Great, am I going to have to cook? I'm so tired, babe.

What do you mean the laundry isn't done? You've been home all day.

How is our power bill so damn high? It's because of your computer. It's sucking up all the electricity.

What do you mean you don't want to have sex tonight? What about what I want?

I let out a heavy sigh, trying to breathe out all my stress and worries. Now that I've had some time away, I can see how unhappy we were together. Everything's so much clearer in hindsight. The resentment in his tone is so much more obvious to me now. If he hadn't hit me, I honestly wonder how much longer we would have lasted.

A soft knock sounds at my door.

"It's open," I say.

Asher steps in, a patient smile on his lips. "Tank's got the car warmed up. Ready to go?"

With a shaky breath, I nod. I just want to get this over with.

"It's going to be an in and out thing," I say, more to myself than to the guys. "Ten minutes, tops."

Beside me, Richard nods. "You can take your time, Winona. There's no need to rush. Better to be thorough so you don't have to come back."

I chew on the inside of my cheek. I've got a mental map drawn out, my keepsakes clear and focused in my mind's eye. The family photo album I left on the bedroom shelf, a few articles of clothing I left behind, some important documents in a small, fire-proof safe tucked away in the closet, and my mother's necklace—the one my father gave to her for their twentieth anniversary. It came into my possession after they passed, a part of my inheritance.

My palms are clammy, my knees bouncing anxiously. Eddie's driving while Tank sits in the passenger seat, actively pointing out street signs and turns as we make our way to my apartment complex. I'm in the back seat in the middle, sandwiched between Richard and Asher. I know things have been kind of rocky between them, but they haven't made comments or thrown pointed glares at each other all day, both too preoccupied with keeping my spirits up.

"It's going to be okay," Asher says, his low voice rumbling in my ear. It's such a pleasant sound it sends a light shiver down my spine and goosebumps crawling over my arms.

When I look down, I see just how close his hand is to mine. It rests on his lap, but the space between us is barely an inch. He offers me his pinky, a quiet and almost timid assurance. I wrap my pinky around his, and we spend the remainder of the ride in silence. We're going to be there soon.

Much to my chagrin, Chet is waiting for us at the front entrance of the building, sitting on the front step leading into the lobby like a guard dog.

"Is that him?" Eddie asks darkly.

I reach out and give his shoulder a light squeeze over the back of his seat. "Behave," I warn.

"No promises, sugar," Tank mumbles, practically a growl.

"I'm serious. There's no telling what Chet might do, but I don't want this ending up with another physical confrontation. One black eye is enough."

The four of them go rigid. My last comment no doubt served as a reminder of what Chet put me through. I wonder if it was a mistake to bring it up, because now all I can sense is bloodlust.

We get out of the car together. Protectiveness must be a contagious affliction because the second my foot touches the pavement, the guys surround me like my own personal guard detail. It makes my insides all warm and gooey knowing I'm in their care. I was dreading this moment, worried about having to face Chet by myself, but with the guys by my side, it doesn't feel nearly as daunting.

Chet rises to his full height. He has at least a foot on me but is still a good couple inches shorter than my bodyguards. The look on his face is hard to decipher. Crestfallen is probably a good word, especially when his eyes lock onto the bruise he so graciously gifted me. There are dark circles under his eyes, which are also puffy and red. His lips are chapped, his hair is greasy, and his shirt is a mess of wrinkles. But the worst part?

The worst part is I feel *bad* for him.

He looks like a kicked puppy left abandoned out in the rain. When he opens his mouth to try and speak, he chokes on a quiet sob. "Winona, I—"

"Shut up," Eddie hisses. "Not a fucking word out of you."

"Stand aside," Asher grumbles.

"No need to make a mountain out of a molehill," Tank adds. "She's just going to grab her stuff and then we're leaving."

Chet's nostrils flare, his face suddenly turning a vibrant red. His lips pull back into a full snarl, his brows pulled together into a steep V. "Who the fuck are you guys?" He tries to reach out to me. "Winona, come the fuck on, this is ridiculous—"

In the blink of an eye, Richard's hand shoots out and snatches Chet by the wrist. "Don't touch her," Richard warns, slow and menacing.

Chet shoots me a look that's equal parts quizzical and enraged. "Who the fuck are they, Winona?"

"They're with me," I say, because I don't owe him anything else. "Don't make a scene, Chet," I say firmly, even though my stomach is two seconds away from bottoming out. Gathering my resolve, I walk right past him and enter the building, Asher, Tank, Eddie, and Richard in tow.

The apartment is in a disheartening state of repair. Evidence of Chet's temper is everywhere. He's put several fist-sized holes in the drywall. The coffee table has been overturned, and at least seven or eight empty beer cans litter the floor. A hurricane could have come through this place and it would have looked neater. I shudder, thinking of the destruction Chet must have rained down after he discovered I left.

"Christ," Tank grumbles as he takes in our surroundings.

Asher puts his hand on the small of my back. The warmth of his palm anchors me in place, keeps me from truly spiraling into despair. "Do you need any help finding your things?"

I shake my head. "I'll be quick. Just... make sure he doesn't get in."

"We got you," Eddie says, his arms crossed defensively over his chest as he glares at the doorway, ready to pounce in an instant.

I move quickly, shuffling through the mess to locate my things. It's frankly a miracle Chet hasn't destroyed my stuff in a fit of rage. There's no time to be delicate with my keepsakes. I grab a plastic bag from the kitchen and shove everything inside, desperate to get the hell out of this place. I feel like at any moment, all I have to do is blink and Chet will appear at the doorway, ready to start a fight again.

Just when I think we're about to make it out of here without a full-on confrontation, Chet forces his way into the apartment, practically charging at Tank like an angry bull. I should have known better than to hope. As fast as lightning, Tank pivots out of the way, snatching Chet by the wrist and using his own momentum against him. Before I know it, Tank has Chet pinned against the nearest wall.

"One wrong move," Tank warns, "and I'll pop your arm right out of your socket."

Chet groans, casting a pleading look my way. "Winona, *please*, just listen to me. I never should have hit you, okay? I know that. I'm really, truly sorry. It'll never happen again, I swear!"

My heart twists angrily in my chest, anguish clawing through my lungs. "How can I possibly believe you?"

"You have to trust me."

"Whatever trust I had in you was shattered the moment you put your hands on me, Chet. I don't think I'll ever feel safe around you again."

Seeing that begging wasn't going to work, the asshole switches tactics. "You won't survive without me, Win. I keep a roof over your head. You barely earn your half of the bills as a freelance editor."

"That's not true. I make more than enough."

"Then why have I been busting my ass at work to provide for you?"

"I never asked to be taken care of, Chet. You made that decision all on your own."

"How do you think you're going to make it without me? Big hot shot with an intern job in New York... You know they don't pay interns, right?"

"That's none of your concern anymore," I insist. "I'll figure it out."

"I give you a week before you come crawling back to me. The city's going to eat you alive."

A terrible pressure is building behind my eyes. I can't take this anymore. "Don't mistake my kindness for weakness, Chet. I'll have you know I'm more than capable of looking after myself."

Asher is by my side, a gentle hand on my upper back. "Let's go, Winona. We got what we came for."

"Don't you dare leave!" Chet screams. "Were you cheating on me with one of these guys this whole time?"

"What are you talking about?"

"That's gotta be it! Why else is it so easy for you to just up and leave me? What, do they all share you or something? Have you been whoring yourself out like some community girlfriend?"

Tank twists Chet's arm until he squeals. "That's about enough of that, asshole. You'll watch your mouth when you talk to her, or you're going to regret it."

"If you leave me, I'll kill myself," Chet screams.

The blood in my veins turns cold. Worse than cold, so heavy and painful my entire body feels like it weighs a thousand pounds. Dread rips through me. I don't know what to say. A part of me wants to dismiss this as a bluff. Surely this is just Chet's last-ditch effort to get me to stay.

But a tiny, insidious voice in the back of my head starts to wonder if he's telling the truth. Will he really hurt himself if I leave? I recognize how fucked up this is, how he's using my emotions against me. It's manipulative as hell and an absolutely shitty thing to do, but on the off chance he's telling the truth... I'm frozen in place, my feet glued to the floor.

"We're leaving," Eddie says, the first to break the silence.

I shake my head, trembling so hard I'm worried I'm about to cave like a house of cards.

"We'll stay with him," Richard states firmly, already in the middle of reaching for his phone. "Tank and I will keep an eye on him while we wait for the police to arrive."

Chet sneers. "The police?"

"Asher, Eddie, take the car and take her home. We'll grab a cab back once we're done here."

Chet struggles against Tank's iron grip. "What the fuck? Let me go!"

"It's okay," Asher whispers in my ear. "Come on, Winona"

I'm too exhausted to argue. I allow Asher and Eddie to lead me away, ignoring Chet's litany of insults and curses as we leave the apartment. Whatever love I had for the man is gone. In less than seventy-two hours, Chet's shown me who he really is—the monstrous things he's capable of.

Eddie drives while Asher sits with me in the back seat. When the car leaves the curb, I begin to cry, sobbing so hard I'm winded and dizzy. Asher wraps his arms around me, his fingers stroking my hair as he mutters sweet words of encouragement in my ear.

"It's okay, Winona. Everything's going to be okay. We're never going to let him hurt you again."

I wholeheartedly believe him.

CHAPTER 7

WINONA

I'm still crying by the time we get back to the lake house. It's not out of fear or sadness, but exhaustion—and maybe a bit of relief. My cries are nothing more than soft whimpers, my eyes so puffy and dry the inside of my skull starts to ache.

Asher hasn't let go of my hand the entire car ride, and I'm quite frankly grateful. Right now, he's my lifeline. If I let go, I'm scared the current might drag me under. Once Eddie's parked the car, he and Asher form up beside me, so I end up walking between them, holding both their hands as we climb the front porch.

Their palms are rough from work, but their grip is tender. While Eddie clasps our hands together, Asher threads his fingers between mine. Such a subtle difference, but the detail doesn't slip past me.

"Why did Richard call the police?" I ask. My voice is frayed from crying.

Eddie fishes for his keys and unlocks the door. "Dude threatened to take his own life. That has to be taken seriously, even if he *is* a piece of shit. No offense."

I shrug my shoulders tiredly. "None taken."

"Richard and Tank will make sure he gets the help he needs," Asher adds. "Regardless of whether or not he was bluffing, they'll stay with him until help arrives."

Despite his kind words, the churning of my stomach won't settle. "What if he really does it? I don't think I could live with myself."

"You are not taking the blame for this," Eddie snaps. His voice is like the sudden beat of a war drum, loud and commanding. "It's just a tactic."

"But what if it's not?"

"Has he ever shown signs of depression before this?"

"Well, no..."

"Has he ever given the impression he might be suicidal?"

"No, never."

"Then this was nothing more than an attempt to manipulate you," Eddie says. "What he chooses to do isn't on you. I've seen how that kind of fuckery works a thousand times. Don't let him win."

I arch a brow, questions echoing around inside my head. "What do you mean, you've seen it a thousand times?"

Eddie sets his jaw, his expression blank, his eyes suddenly cold and distant. "Nothing," he murmurs before heading down the hall. He disappears into his room, the soft click of his door shutting behind him somehow twice as loud in my ear.

When I shoot Asher a curious glance, he simply shakes his head. "Not my story to tell. The point is, you're out now. That was our top priority."

I manage a small, albeit stiff smile. I'm just so damn tired, and I'm really starting to hate it. I had no idea just how much energy Chet was draining out of me. I'm finally free, and it feels like a massive ton of bricks has lifted off my shoulders. I have to admit it's going to take some getting used to. All this freedom is both exhilarating and intimidating.

"You did very well," Asher says, looking at me with a warm softness in his eyes. "That could have been a lot messier, but you did good holding your own."

A delightful shiver whispers down my spine at the praise. "Thanks, but I can't take all the credit. I don't think I could have done it without the four of you there to back me up."

"It's like Eddie said, we got you."

We got you.

Three easy syllables, yet it's so complicated. I don't know when it happened, but I've started to feel like a part of this little unit of theirs. I feel closer to the four of them than I have with Chet over the entirety of our four-year relationship. It's crazy. Almost impossible, but I know they feel it, too.

What, do they all share you or something?

Heat lances through my belly. What a strange, yet delicious thought to entertain. I was in such shock when Chet first made the comment, I wrote it off as nothing more than slander. But now that I've finally had a chance to cool down, there's something oddly appealing about the idea of being—well, *shared*.

I don't know where my head's at, but I can't bring myself to stop. It goes without question that I think Asher, Tank, Eddie, and Richard are incredibly sexy. Each one of them brings a little something different to the table, a different flavor I'm dying to bite into.

My heart thuds nervously in my chest. This is such a silly fantasy, but I can't stop thinking about the four of them surrounding me, about their lips and how they'd feel on my skin, or the way their rough hands could explore my body—all at the exact same time. After all the shit Chet's put me through, after hurting me physically and emotionally, is it so bad to want to feel cherished and loved and wanted?

It hits me again just how free I am. I can do whatever I want, whatever pleases me.

"Winona?"

The sound of Asher's voice breaks me from my daydream. My cheeks flush with heat. I must be tired to be fantasizing about four men right in front of one of them. Feeling caught in the act, I try laughing it off. "Sorry, I was just, uh... thinking."

He chuckles as he reaches out, easily tucking a few strands of my hair behind my ear. Asher's knuckles graze my cheek, his smile so dashing I momentarily forget how to breathe. "You've had a long day. Why don't you go lie down?"

I nibble on my bottom lip and watch as his eyes slide down to follow the motion. Am I going crazy, or has Asher stopped breathing, too? Would it be so terrible if I took a step forward, closed the gap between us, and finally—

Asher makes the first move, easily crowding me against the wall behind me as his fingers comb through my hair. His lips claim mine with far more ferocity than I thought he was capable of. His kisses are a complete contrast to his otherwise sweet and caring nature—rough and domineering and insatiable.

I instinctively grab him by the shirt collar, keeping his body anchored to mine. He's so nice and solid against me I can feel the hard lines of his rolling muscles beneath taut skin. Asher grinds his hips against mine with a low growl. The unmistakable press of his arousal against my belly causes a soft whimper to bubble past my lips. Heat pools between my legs.

"*Oh*," I rasp, clinging to him. "Asher—"

"Do you want me to stop?" he mutters against the crook of my neck. His breath is hot and heavy against my skin.

"No, don't stop. It's just..."

Click.

I look to my left down the hall and find Eddie planted in the middle of the hall, watching Asher and me with... I can't tell, actually. My initial reaction is one of guilt, attempting to squirm away from Asher's hold. He only holds me tighter.

Eddie's eyes darken. I don't detect any anger or jealousy.

Only hunger.

"Kiss her again," he says, stalking toward us like a wolf getting ready to pounce. "I want to hear her make that noise again."

At first, I think Asher might step away. Does Eddie not realize what he's asking? He wants to... *watch?* My heart is officially beating loudly in my throat, my knees shaking and my thoughts a jumble. My body burns so hot I fear I might burst into an inferno. And just when I think I can't get any more confused—

Asher kisses me again. Harder this time.

He sucks on my bottom lip, dragging his teeth over it. His hold is so tight our bodies have no choice but to crush together. I've never been kissed with this kind of passion, have never been held with this much need. And even more mind blowing is the fact that Eddie sidles up beside me, brushes my hair away from my face, and moves in to nibble on my ear.

I'm suddenly overwhelmed by them, their mouths exploring at two different speeds. Where Asher kisses like we have to make up for lost time, Eddie is unhurried and surprisingly gentle. I fully expected this big, gruff, perpetually scowling man to want to devour me. Instead, he handles me like I'm made of fine crystals, so tender and sweet it almost makes me cry.

A moan rips from my lungs. I barely recognize the sound of my own voice, the blood rushing past my ears making it nearly impossible to hear. Someone's hand slides from my hip to my thighs, gripping with even pressure. Someone else's hand slides up to my breast, giving it a squeeze. I close my eyes, lost to the sensations of pleasure pulsing through me. This is better than I thought it would be, and although I have no idea what's happening or how we got here, I decide to enjoy the ride.

"Touch me," I whimper, taking Eddie's hand to guide it down to my thighs.

He obliges, rubbing his palm over my aching core. Eddie hums contently, kissing the corner of my mouth in a light, teasing manner. "Look at Asher, sweetheart. Let him see how turned on you are."

My eyes lock onto Asher, marveling at the lust in his heated gaze. Eddie's hand slips down the waistband of my pants, slips past my underwear, until his fingers finally graze my sensitive clit. I fail to hold back a gasping moan, gripping Asher's shoulders as my mouth falls open in pleasure.

"You're so fucking beautiful," Asher growls. "Ain't that right, Eddie?"

"Fuck, yes," he murmurs against my cheek. "Does that feel good, sweetheart?"

Time and space lose all meaning. I can't believe this is happening. Surely this has to be a dream, right? I thought maybe there'd be some awkwardness, but Asher and Eddie don't seem the least bit bothered, perfectly content to turn all their attention and affection toward me.

"Your room or mine?" Asher asks Eddie.

"Who's got the bigger bed?"

"W-wait!" I interject, thoroughly flustered.

"What is it, angel?"

I gulp, my throat dry and my head spinning. "Are you sure we should..."

"Is this not what you want?" Asher asks.

"No, I want this. Believe me, I want this. It's just... What about Tank and Richard?"

"What *about* Tank and Richard?" Eddie asks gruffly. After a moment, his lips stretch into a devilish grin. "Ah, I see... Our girl's greedy."

"I-I am not!" I stammer. "I just—"

Asher chuckles. "He's teasing you."

"Oh."

Eddie kisses my cheek sweetly. "Tell you what, sweetheart... Why don't the three of us have some fun, and when Tank and Richard get back, we'll talk to them."

My stomach flips, my hands trembling with adrenaline. "Really? Do you think they'd... Is this something they would..."

Asher licks his lips and smiles. "Fuck, you're cute when you're flustered. Eddie and I will talk to them, okay? For now, though, you should probably pick a bedroom."

I let out a slow exhale, looking between Asher and Eddie in search of any signs of doubt. Are we in over our heads here? Is this even a good idea? But I can't help what my body wants, and right now it needs them on top of me, behind me, inside me.

"Mine," I finally answer. "Let's go to mine."

CHAPTER 8

ASHER

As far as threesomes go, I have no experience whatsoever. A sane man probably would have bailed, but I trust Eddie. We've had each other's backs for years. We've shared the same foxholes and dwindling rations and rotated a single machine gun between the two of us. Sharing is not an issue.. There's no awkwardness, no need for talk. Eddie and I have worked together for so long we're in tune with each other.

Our mission is loud and clear: Winona, and only Winona.

Eddie carries her to bed, depositing her as carefully as he would fine China. It's strange, seeing him this gentle. Winona must bring it out in him, and I'm certainly not complaining. If he's going to be tender with her, maybe I can be a little rough.

We quickly join her on the bed, the mattress creaking under our combined weight. My mouth finds hers with ease, two comets destined to collide. I love the sounds she makes, so breathy and soft and desperate they ignite something almost feral inside of me. It takes every ounce of my willpower not to tear her clothes right off. I have to remind myself that we have time. There's nothing wrong with savoring the moment.

I undress her, one article of clothing at a time, while Eddie keeps her occupied with his lips. I memorize every inch of skin I expose, charting every peak and valley and plain of her body a whole new world to discover.

Winona seems just as eager to undress us, tugging at our shirts and fumbling with our belts. She huffs in frustration when she has to choose one or the other, moving back and forth between Eddie and me like a child lost in a candy shop with too many options to choose from. She even whines into the next kiss I give her, impatience radiating off her in waves.

"Take it easy, angel," I chide. "We're not going anywhere."

"Just relax," Eddie murmurs.

I scoot behind her and wrap my arms around her smaller frame. I lavish her in kisses, my tongue sweeping over hers without mercy. The heat of her body and the taste of her mouth are nothing short of divine, so sweet and overwhelming it's enough to blank my mind. At this moment, nothing else is as important as her soft, languid moans or the way she scrapes her nails through my hair.

Eddie makes his way down, peppering a line of kisses to her breasts, her stomach, her hips. He grips her milky thighs hard enough that his fingers leave divots on her skin, pushing her knees apart to expose her pussy.

"Fuck, you taste so good, sweetheart," Eddie grunts against her core.

"I can't wait to try," I murmur against her lips.

"Wait your turn."

Winona laughs, breathy and light. "No need to figh—" A deep moan rips from her lungs as Eddie redoubles his efforts, licking and teasing her senseless. Trembles wrack her body, her back arching as she whimpers.

I swallow the sounds, relishing the way she holds onto me, the sheets, anything she can get those greedy little hands on. My cock strains against the confines of my boxers, throbbing with need. These little sounds of hers are going to drive me up the wall, and if I don't find a way to relieve some of the pressure, this whole endeavor is going to be embarrassingly short.

So while I kiss the ever-loving daylights out of her, I take her hand and guide it down to my cock, slipping the waistband of my boxers down below my balls. "Go on, angel. Touch all you want."

When she wraps her long, soft fingers around my shaft I nearly lose my mind. She strokes gently at first, testing the waters. And while I delight in her caution and care, I want so much more than her shy touch. So I wrap my own hand around hers and guide her, helping to give her a sense of what I'm after. She seems delighted and surprised at the speed and roughness, but quickly falls into rhythm, eagerly jerking me off while my tongue glides over hers.

"Good girl," I murmur. "Just like that."

"Eddie—"

"What is it, angel?"

Winona whines. "I'm *close.*"

From between her thighs, I hear Eddie chuckle. "Go on, sweetheart. I want you to come on my tongue."

She doesn't hold back. With a few rapid breaths, Winona comes undone, crying out as pleasure claims her. She's truly a sight to behold, far more beautiful than I can ever hope to comprehend. I like the flush of her cheeks, her neck, and her chest. I adore the way she squeezes Eddie's face between her trembling thighs. Her lips are so plump and swollen, delectable in every way.

Her pleasure is addicting.

And I'm about to become a very willing user.

"Move over," I say gruffly, my voice huskier than usual. "I want to see how loud I can make her scream."

Eddie helps Winona sit up, her arms circling his neck as he pulls her upright into his lap. Their kiss is so sweet and tender, lazy and perfect. But I feel no jealousy, no rage when I see Winona's lips on another man. All I care about is the way she smiles and melts into Eddie's touch, totally at ease. I wouldn't have it any other way.

He leans back and takes Winona along with him. She has her

hands braced on either side of his head while her knees are spread, legs straddling him. I slowly drag my fingers down the length of her back, adoring how she shivers beneath my touch. I give her peachy ass a good clap, sucking in a sharp breath through my gritted teeth.

"Are you on anything, angel?"

"The pill," she rasps.

"I can try and find a condom if you want extra protection."

"No," she says quickly. "No, I don't want anything between us. I want to feel you deep inside me, Asher."

Her sultry voice and dirty words make my cock throb. I *need* to be inside her. So I settle on my knees behind her, grip her harshly by the thighs, and align myself with her entrance. "You're sure this is what you want, Winona?" I ask one more time.

She looks over her shoulder at me, her eyes dark and burning with lust. "Do your worst."

Eddie chuckles.

I lick my lips. I can't wait anymore.

I bury myself into her tight, wet pussy, savoring her high-pitched gasp. Her walls clench around me, pulsing, almost sucking me in deeper. It's Heaven on Earth. Winona takes me so well, I swear to God she must have been made for me.

I snap my hips against her roughly, driving myself into her pussy with a low grunt. Winona half-moans, half-laughs. It's such a delightful sound. I want to hear it again, so I thrust into her over and over, rougher and faster each time. I don't know what's gotten into me. I'm entranced by the way she feels, hypnotized by her siren voice. There isn't a single rational thought left inside my head except for how much I want to make this woman come on my cock.

Beneath me, Winona shakes and pants and whimpers, held in place by Eddie's strong grasp, and her desperate cries of 'yes, please, right there, fuck me harder' spur me on. She likes it rough—and I'm going to give her exactly what she needs.

Pistoning in and out of her, I reach down and grab a fistful of her hair, pulling her head back gently but firmly to keep control of our pace. The moment her neck is exposed, Eddie kisses her throat, sucking hard enough to leave marks all over her pale skin. While I fuck her from behind, he squeezes her breasts and teases her nipples between his fingers.

"A-Asher, I'm—*ah*—I'm going to—"

"Come on my cock, angel." I thrust into her hard.

She screams when climax takes her, shattering around me like a firework. The walls of her pussy flutter, the clench of her around my cock sending me hurtling over the edge. I've never had an orgasm quite like this. It's explosive and brilliant, so powerful it momentarily leaves me winded. I'm all things satiated and adrenaline and content, the lava coursing through my veins inexplicably hot, but fleeting.

No sooner than I finish, Eddie immediately rolls Winona onto her back, nudging her legs apart so he can slide into her. I lay down at her side, kissing her tenderly as I stroke my fingers through her hair, while Eddie fucks her gently. I didn't know the guy was capable of being so careful, but Winona certainly doesn't seem to have any complaints. He treats her like a damn princess, and frankly, it's what she deserves after the workout I just gave her.

"So fucking beautiful," Eddie grumbles as he rolls his hips. "Fuck, Winona, I want—"

"Yes?" she asks, cupping his face in her hands. "Tell me, what do you want?"

All it takes is one look at his face and I know exactly what he's thinking. I've known the guy for so long it's easy to tell, like reading the pages of an open book. I chuckle, pressing my lips to her shoulder. "He wants to come inside you."

"Can I?" Eddie groans.

Winona nods. "Yes! Yes, please."

The sound of pure bliss, followed by a welcome stillness fills the room. Eddie rolls to the side, placing Winona between us on the bed. The sheets are crumpled, pillows askew, but there is nothing more gorgeous than the gentle rise and fall of Winona's chest as she wears a dopey smile. She holds our hands, one on either side, as she giggles softly to herself. What I wouldn't give to bottle up the sound and keep it with me forever.

"Wow," she says, breathing out slowly. Her eyelids droop, heavy with sleep.

I press a kiss to her temple, chuckling. "That was amazing."

Eddie kisses her opposite cheek. "Perfection," he agrees.

"What happens now?" she whispers.

"You close your eyes and get some rest," I say, "and we'll talk to the guys when they get here."

Winona nibbles on her bottom lip. "Do you think they'll be weirded out?"

Eddie shakes his head. "I doubt it."

"Just let us handle it," I tell her firmly. "Don't worry about a thing, angel."

When I peer into her eyes, I see no hesitation, no doubt. She trusts us, and there's no more proof of that than when her eyes slowly close and she falls into a deep, well-deserved sleep.

CHAPTER 9

TANK

Well, *that's three and a half hours of my life I'm never getting back.*

Chet made a huge stink once the cops showed up, but what else were we supposed to do? I don't much care for the bastard, but Richard and I weren't about to risk leaving him alone in case the idiot decided to follow through with his threat. It was a load off my mind when Asher and Eddie took Winona home, because things frankly got ugly after she left.

The cussing, the spitting...

The threats on her life.

"Sir, you need to come with us," the officer said as he ushered Chet toward the back of his police vehicle.

"You can't keep me from her!" he seethes. "She's mine, do you understand? She really thinks she can leave me? I'll fucking kill her before that happens!"

My nostrils flare, rage coursing through my veins. "You son of a—"

Richard nabs me by my good shoulder, preventing me from taking another step forward. "Stand down," he orders. We may not be on active duty, but I respect his command regardless. It's just as well. I'm two seconds away from losing it on Chet, and I don't feel like being arrested for homicide—though I'm pretty confident I can make it look like an accident.

The miserable fucker calls us every name under the sun as the cops lead him away. Causing a public disturbance, utterance of death threats, stinking up the very air we breathe with his presence—I don't know what charges are going to stick, but I sincerely hope this is the last time we have to see him. Not just for Winona's sake, but for his. If I ever lay eyes on him again, if he comes anywhere near Winona...

I won't be able to control myself.

It takes another twenty minutes of being interviewed by the police before we're finally allowed to leave. Richard and I try to recount everything to the best of our abilities. We're not the ones in trouble here, but with the way we're being interrogated, it sure feels like we are.

"And where is the ex-girlfriend now?" the cop asks us.

"She's staying with us."

"What's your relationship with the woman?"

My eye twitches. "We're her brother's friends."

"And you all live together?" There's a whole lot of judgment dripping off his words. I don't appreciate it.

"Temporarily," Richard answers evenly. Leave it to our captain to remain level-headed, even at a time like this.

"I'd like to speak to her."

I bristled. Winona's been through enough today. "For what purpose? We told you everything that happened."

The officer sighs. "I need to know if this is a pattern of behavior. If she wants a restraining order. That sort of thing."

"She's already been taken home," Richard answers bluntly.

The officer claps his notebook shut. "If anything comes up, have her give us a call."

"Does this mean we're free to go?" I ask.

He nods with a grunt and stalks off. I'm personally relieved. All I want is to get back to the lake house and make sure Winona's okay. I can't explain this strange tightness in my chest when I think about her. What is she thinking? How is she feeling? What can I do to make her feel alright? She has me under some sort of spell—and I'm definitely not complaining.

The cab ride home is long and silent. I can tell Richard is a lot angrier than he's letting on. He's always been good at that, keeping his emotions in check and his face unreadable, but I've known the man for a decade. It's all about knowing where to look. Richard carries his anger in the tension of his shoulders, his annoyance in the tight clench of his jaw. I can tell he's just as anxious to get back to the lake house as I am.

When we finally arrive, we pay the cab driver and head inside. It's oddly quiet. I know Winona, Asher, and Eddie must be back because my car's parked out front. There's no shuffling around in the kitchen, no TV on in the living room... What the hell is going on here?

"We're back!" I call out, my voice echoing off the walls.

"Maybe they went out for a walk?" Richard suggests.

Our questions are answered when we hear the creak of a door opening somewhere down the hall, followed by the soft padding of feet against the hardwood floors. Asher walks towards us dressed in nothing but his underwear. His hair is wild and a light sheen of sweat covers his shoulders and chest...

But even more apparent are the claw marks down his arms and the self-satisfied grin he wears.

"You made it," he says, very much the cat who got the cream.

"And what have you been up to?" I ask, arching a brow.

Asher tilts his head in the opposite direction, guiding us.

Curious, my feet carry me forward before my brain has the chance to register what I'm seeing. Why is Asher headed straight for Winona's room? Once we're at the open doorway, I understand why in an instant.

Winona's in bed, curled up against Eddie's chest, fast asleep. And very, *very* naked. Eddie has the audacity to throw up a pair of deuces, his smirk both amusing and frustrating me at the same time because *what the hell?*

I glance between Asher and Eddie, confused for only a moment. "Hold your horses, did you two..."

Asher's smile widens. It's like he's celebrating his birthday and Christmas all at once. "She felt bad because the two of you weren't here to join the fun."

My heart rattles inside my rib cage, blood rushing with such force through my veins it leaves me dizzy. "She... said that?"

It's certainly a lot to process. There's no denying how much I'm attracted to her, and I sort of got the sense Winona liked each of us equally, but I never could have imagined... *sharing* her with the other guys. The more I turn the think about it, however, the more I grow used to the idea.

Seeing her in Eddie's arms, seeing the marks on Asher's skin... It doesn't fill me with jealousy or rage. If anything, I'm happy for her. Happy she could find satisfaction and pleasure; happy my brothers could take care of her while I was away. And it pleases me to no end knowing Winona might be interested in having Richard and me, too. What was the term Chet used earlier today? A *community girlfriend.*

I see nothing wrong with it. There's more than enough love to go around, and plenty of fun to be had. If this is what she wants, I'm sure as hell not going to be a stick in the mud. I'm confident enough that I don't feel the need to compare myself to the other guys. What man could ever say no to an opportunity like this?

"You fucking idiots," Richard grumbles. "What have you done?"

"What do you mean?" Asher asks, crossing his arms.

"This is wrong. That's William's little sister and he told us to look after her, not seduce her."

Asher sighs, closing the door behind him slowly so as to not disturb Winona. "Look, she wants this. *We* want this. I've seen the way you look at her, don't try to deny it."

"It's dishonorable," Richard growls. "We made William a promise to look after her."

"And we are. Just... not in a traditional sense."

"She's ten years younger than all of you," he counters. "And *fifteen* years younger than me."

The discussion is getting heated, so I step in between them. "You can't forget she's a grown adult capable of making her own choices."

Richard shoots me a quizzical look. "Not you, too. I expected better of you, Tank."

I set my jaw. "Listen, Judge Judy, no one's forcing you to do anything if you don't want to. But you have to take into consideration Winona's wishes—"

"She's in a vulnerable place right now. She just left her abusive ex, for fuck's sake."

"Why are you being such an asshole?" Asher grumbles. "Ever since we got back, you've been nothing but a pain in the ass."

"I'm trying to do what's best for her," Richard counters. "And you know as well as I do I've been looking into what happened. What *I* don't understand is how you can all be so nonchalant about it. We failed our mission. We lost good men, and all you three can think about is—"

"What's going on?" a soft voice cuts through our argument.

The three of us turn to see Winona at the doorway, the bed sheets wrapped around her body for warmth. She looks prettier than a dream, her hair curling over her exposed shoulders with love bites adorning her neck. It drives me crazy knowing Asher and Eddie got to have their fun. Eddie is behind her, fully nude. It doesn't bother me in the slightest. It's perfunctory, really. What I *really* want to see is Winona splayed out beneath me, every inch of her body mine to claim.

"Are you two fighting?" Winona asks, her brows knitting together as she looks between Asher and Richard.

I've never seen Richard so uncomfortable. It's not an expression I thought he was capable of. He's normally so in control and powerful.

Winona's simple question and wide eyes are apparently all it takes to make him unravel.

"We dealt with your ex," Richard mutters. "He won't be bothering you anymore."

"Dealt with?" she echoes.

"I'm going to my room."

"Richard—"

He retreats too quickly for any of us to react. I've always respected the man, but I kind of hate him right now for leaving Winona in the lurch. There's nothing I want to do more than wipe away the disappointment weighing down her features.

"I freaked him out, didn't I?" she mumbles.

Eddie combs his fingers through her hair, dipping down to press his lips to her shoulder. I've never seen him more at peace. "Don't worry about it, sweetheart."

I can't hold back any longer. Winona is a tempting treat, dangling herself in front of me like this. With my good hand, I reach out and stroke her cheek, the sensation of her soft skin against my palms suddenly washing away all my worries. "It looks like you've had an eventful afternoon. Mind if I join in?"

Her worry melts away, a sweet smile slowly brightening her gorgeous face. "You really want to? It doesn't weird you out?"

"No, sugar. If anything, it's going to bring out my competitive streak."

"How so?"

I smirk. "How many times did they make you come?"

Winona's cheeks flush pink. "Oh, uh... I wasn't counting."

"I'll just have to come up with a number myself then. And double it."

"What about your arm?" she asks with a giggle. "I don't want you to hurt yourself, Tank."

"Hm... I suppose you're right. I guess you're just going to have to ride me like a cowgirl, sugar."

CHAPTER 10

WINONA

W here Asher's kisses are rough and breathtaking, and Eddie's kisses sweet and tender, Tank's kisses are downright playful and teasing.

"Are you sure we shouldn't check on Richard?" I ask.

"Let him sulk," Tank says as he peppers my cheek with light pecks. I adore how they tickle. "I want your eyes on me."

It would be easy to let my troubles fall away now that I have Asher, Tank, and Eddie's undivided attention, but the butterflies in my stomach won't settle. I must have taken Richard by surprise. I feel a little guilty for walking out in nothing more than my bedsheets, but that look he gave me... It's so obvious he wants me, maybe even more than the other guys, but for some reason, he won't act on it.

We failed our mission. We lost good men, and all you three can thinking about is—

I want to know what happened, but I also don't want to force him to answer. Whatever it is, it sounds serious, but do I dare pry?

Unfortunately—or perhaps fortunately—I'm too distracted by Tank's lips on mine, Asher's teeth grazing my shoulder, and Eddie's fingers curling in my hair. Going after Richard will just have to wait. Right now, I'm about to have the time of my life. *Again.*

Eddie tugs the bed sheet away from my body, leaving me exposed to their ravenous eyes. Tank looks pleased as punch, drinking me in like a man stranded in the desert.

"Good Lord," he murmurs to himself.

I can't help but giggle. "Like what you see?"

"Are you kidding? I think you're about to give me a heart attack."

"Quit yapping," Eddie grumbles, "or I'm taking my turn first."

"Like hell you are."

I throw my head back and laugh.

The corners of Tank's lips tug up into an amused smile. "Mind helping me with my belt?"

"With pleasure."

It's a treat and a half undressing Tank because of his sheer size. Everything about him is so massive there's no shortage of skin for my eyes to delight in. First go his pants, then I carefully undo the buttons of his shirt. My gaze falls to his impressive bulge, my mouth watering on instinct. Without being asked, I drop to my knees and drag the waistband of his black boxer briefs down with me.

To say Tank is well endowed is an understatement. Honestly, what did I expect? It only makes sense that a man his size would have an impressive cock to match. My only concern is—

"Will it even fit?" I ask aloud.

"It will," he says with the utmost confidence. "Now, show me what that pretty mouth of yours can do."

I wrap my lips around the head of his dick and take in the salty taste of his skin. The weight of his erection on my tongue is like nothing I've experienced, hot and heavy and utterly divine.

Tank squeezes his eyes shut and moans. "Goddamn that's good."

"Don't forget about us, sweetheart," Eddie murmurs, casually striding closer. He dips down to guide my hand toward his throbbing length, a smile of approval upon his lips.

I feel drunk, simultaneously intoxicated and high off their attention. I can't remember the last time I felt this adored. They spoil me with sweet words of encouragement, stroke my hair, and keep their eyes on me. It's equal parts overwhelming and addicting. Chet was never this attentive, more of a taker than a giver, and now that I've had a taste of what I've been missing for four years, I don't see myself stopping any time soon.

"Bring her here," Asher says, making his way over to my bed.

Eddie picks me up and throws me over his shoulder. I can't help but let out a yelp as my legs flail about and I grip his shoulders for support. He chuckles, the sound so rare and precious it's like I've stumbled into a treasure trove full of gold.

Tank settles down on the mattress, leaning against my pillows and the headrest. Eddie deposits me onto Tank's lap, and I handle things from there. I straddle him, mindful of his injured arm. I do pause for a moment as I gaze at his scars. They're still bright pink, the injury only a few weeks old. Some areas are still covered in gauze and bandages.

"I don't want to hurt you," I tell him softly.

"I'm tougher than I look."

"You'll tell me if it gets to be too much, right?"

"You got it, sugar."

With my hands braced against the headboard, I slowly lower myself onto Tank's length, closing my eyes as I savor the pleasure-pinch of the stretch. I have to take a couple of deep breaths, moving as slowly as I can to give myself time to adjust. He's patient with me, dragging his teeth over my bottom lip as he kisses me.

Asher is kneeling on his knees directly behind me, mouthing hungrily at the crook of my neck with his hands on either side of my waist. He helps me lower myself, providing the support I need to welcome Tank all the way in. Once I'm ready, I begin to move, slowly raising and lowering myself with Asher's help.

It's definitely a workout, but the burn in my muscles and in my lungs is deeply gratifying. Like I've dived head-first into a ten-mile marathon and everything is in peak condition, all my senses working together. I lose myself in the heat of Asher's chest against my back, his cock rubbing against my ass, all the while Tank's languid moans of pleasure send my mind into a tailspin.

"Fuck, you feel so good," Tank groans.

"You're so beautiful," Asher mumbles against my cheek. His hands wrap around to squeeze at my breasts, gently pinching my pebbled nipples between his fingers. "I love the way you move, angel."

"Brush her hair out of her face," Eddie grumbles his order. He's seated on the edge of the bed, back twisted slightly to watch us, his hand between his legs to slowly stroke his arousal. I'm convinced there's nothing more erotic than the way he's looking at me right now, thoroughly transfixed on my face as he pleasures himself.

Asher nibbles on my earlobe as he combs my hair away with his fingers, his voice a low growl in my ear. I don't know what I'm supposed to concentrate on most. The feeling of Tank deep inside me, the burning sensation of Asher's hands all over my body, or the way Eddie's gaze burrows into my soul.

All of a sudden, it feels like I'm floating five feet off the ground. Pleasure grips me tight, explosive and dangerous and exhilarating. Sounds and lights blur, motions come slower as time comes to a stand-still while Tank empties himself deep inside me. Before I can register what's happening, Asher is helping me off Tank's lap before he promptly pins my back to the mattress.

He's on top of me like a lion, his ferocious mouth marking my skin. He settles between my thighs and slips into me, thrusting in and out at an impressive speed. A sharp gasp knocks from my lungs when the head of his cock sweeps over my sweet spot. Electricity sparks through my veins, leaving every inch of my body exposed like a live wire.

"Right there?" he asks with a chuckle.

I nod quickly, dragging my nails down his muscular back. "Yes! Yes, right there!"

Asher makes my pleasure his mission, aiming for my sweet spot over and over and over until I unravel beneath him, stars twinkling across my vision. I'm breathing so hard it makes me dizzier. Every muscle fiber in my body is nothing more than putty, worked and kneaded into a state of complete relaxation.

The only reason I know Asher's finished is because he switches places with Eddie, who's been patiently observing from his side of the bed. Eddie greets me with a deep, slow, sensual kiss, his tongue gliding over mine with unhurried ease.

"Catch your breath," he murmurs against my lips. "Easy does it, sweetheart. You're so fucking gorgeous."

"Eddie..."

He holds me like he's never going to let go, arms locked on either side of me as he buries himself between my thighs. I'm starting to learn that with Eddie, every single one of his thoughts can be conveyed through his eyes. Just a look. That's all I need to know how he's feeling, what he wants, how he plans to take me slow and sweet.

When his hand slides down between us to rub my sensitive clit, I'm a goner. Wave after wave of pure bliss wracks my body, and all I can do is hold onto his shoulders for dear life. Eddie isn't very far behind me, because after a few hard pumps of his hips, he eventually stills.

I'm already starting to drift off, positioned snugly in the middle of the bed between the three men. Someone presses a kiss to my hair, someone else wraps me in the blanket for warmth, and someone murmurs sweet nothings in my ear as sleep pulls me under.

CHAPTER 11

EDDIE

We're just about to breach the front door of the compound—
A bomb goes off.
I'm surrounded by rubble and dust, my ears ringing so loudly I fear my
head will explode—just like Reiko's. He was supposed to be first
through the door, but now he lies on the ground in pieces. The thick
scent of iron lingers in the air, coating my tongue and burning the
insides of my nostrils.
Asher's yelling at me. I can't tell what he's saying; the pressure inside
my skull is too intense to focus on the sound of his voice.
Tank is beside me on the ground, distressingly still. His right arm is in
shambles, red soaking through his uniform.
I don't know where Richard is. I'm worried he's dead. Just like
Jameson and Fischer behind me—blown to bits.
Through the dust, I can see movement. Someone's coming. They're
armed, their sights trained on us. We're sitting ducks now. Easy
pickings.
Gunfire. I try to move, but my body won't cooperate. My legs are lead,
my lungs full of concrete. This is it. I'm done for.
But I don't want to die.

~

"**E**ddie!"

Someone grabs me by the shoulder. I react with force, hopped up on so much adrenaline I can't tell my dreams from my waking nightmare. I throttle the man by the throat, rolling us out of bed with such speed there's no time to catch ourselves.

We land on the hardwood floor with a heavy *thud*. The guy's on top of me, wrestling my hands away from his face. Pain shrieks through my spine where I landed, but I don't give up. I'm not going to let this motherfucker kill me.

"Eddie!" Asher bellows. "For fuck's sake, snap out of it!"

I can't.

There's a fog over my mind. I can hear Asher's voice, I can see him above me, trying to shake me from the hold of my nightmare, but no matter how hard I try, I can't snap back to reality. I don't want to hurt him, but fear has gripped me so tight can no longer distinguish friend from foe. I'm trapped inside my own head, helpless and alone and paralyzed. The harder I try to scream, the more my chest wants to cave in.

"What's going on?" I think it's Richard. Out of my periphery, I can see he's at the door, bursting through in alarm.

"We can't get him to wake up," Tank tells him.

"Eddie?" A much softer, sweeter voice reaches my ears.

"Stay back, Winona," Richard warns.

But she doesn't. Instead, she hops out of bed and kneels beside me, cupping my face in her hands. Her fingers are cool to the touch, refreshing. Slowly but surely, I feel the tension in my body melting. Asher's hold on me loosens and Winona takes his place beside me, her forehead pressed firmly against mine.

"Look at me, Eddie," she whispers. "Look at me."

Instinct tells me not to. Danger is everywhere. I have to stay alert, can't afford to break focus. But as my breathing calms and Winona gently repeats my name, I can feel my mind slowly come back to reality. I finally find the strength to look up at her, breathing in the scent of roses and peaches. Her beauty, her kindness—it breaks my heart. Someone so wonderful can't possibly be a part of my nightmare.

"Take a deep breath," she coos. "It's okay. You're safe. We've got you, Eddie."

And I believe her.

Winona presses a kiss to the corner of my mouth, my cheek, the tip of my nose. There isn't a hint of judgment in her eyes, only concern for my well-being.

I glance at Asher once my breathing has calmed down. "Did I hurt you?"

He shakes his head. "No. Don't worry about it, brother."

I return my attention to Winona, my hands still shaking as I grasp her gently by the arms. "Did I hurt *you*?"

Winona smiles gently. "No. I'm totally fine."

My throat is dry, my heart twisting angrily between my ribs. That was a close call. Too close. What if I'd attacked Winona in my panic? What if I had hurt her? I don't think I could ever forgive myself.

I help Winona to her feet, doing my best to swallow my embarrassment. *Fuck.* The guys are all looking at me with a wash of pity and I can't stand it.

"Eddie," Richard says slowly. "Get dressed. Let's take some air."

I grit my teeth. "I'm fine."

Tank hits me with a stern look. "Eddie, maybe you should—"

"I said I'm fine!" I grab my clothes from the floor and start toward the door. "I'll go back to my room so you can sleep."

Winona's mouth opens as if to say something, but I leave before she can get a word out. Richard follows; I should have known that he would.

"There's nothing wrong asking for help," Richard tells me. "It's not a weakness, Luna."

I make it to my room at the other end of the hall, my grip on the doorknob so tight my fingers ache. I don't know what to say, so I don't. Ignoring him, I enter my room and shut the door firmly behind me.

The digital alarm clock on my bedside table reads 5:48 a.m. I'll be getting up in a couple of hours anyway, and I'd much rather not go back to sleep, so I hop into the shower to wash off the remnants of my dream. My memories sit heavily in my gut, so bitter and violent it threatens to make me throw up.

I let the shower run on cold and step under the stream, the water so frigid it shocks my entire system awake. It kind of hurts; the tips of my fingers and toes are throbbing as the icy spray numbs my skin.

It's not a weakness, Luna.

I'm more than aware of that, but I can't bring myself to seek help. Is it because I'm still in denial? Like if I go speak to someone about my trauma, it's like I'm admitting the horrors I witnessed that day really happened? Because the more I think about it, the more insane I feel. It's no wonder Richard's been so adamant about getting to the root of the problem. Everything was going according to plan...

Until it wasn't.

Richard's right. It was an off-the-books job. Literally only our team and our immediate supervisor knew about the operation. It was supposed to be an in and out deal. All we had to do was infiltrate, nab our target, and bring the person in for questioning. Our location was a secret, as was the time of our strike. So how the fuck did they know we were coming?

I'm telling you someone sold us out!

Three good men are dead, Tank's injured, and I'm fucked up in the head. Richard and Asher, normally so in sync and the closest of friends, can barely stand to be in the same room together. Someone somewhere must have planned this, planned for us to fall apart. The more I turn these thoughts over in my head, the more I realize Richard is right.

I doubt any one of us is a rat, which leaves only one option.

Colonel George Grey, our commanding officer and Asher's grandfather. If he was the one who turned on us, the four of us are in big trouble.

The only question is *why?*

CHAPTER 12

WINONA

"How're you doing, kiddo?" William asks, bright and chipper over the phone.

He called shortly after breakfast, though I'm frankly thankful for the distraction. Between dealing with Richard's distance and Eddie's grumpiness, tensions are running higher than usual. I practically leapt at the chance to answer my phone, excusing myself to take it outside on the porch.

"It's going good," I answer, taking in the morning sunshine off the surface of the lake. "How are things in Seattle?"

"Rainy as hell, but who's surprised? I'm sorry I didn't call you earlier. Things have been crazy."

"Business is good, I take it?"

"I think I might have three new investors on board," William says. I can practically hear the smile in his voice.

"That's great!" I tell him, genuinely excited. "You'll be on the cover of *Forbes* one of these days."

My brother chuckles. "You flatterer. But enough about me. How are the boys treating you? They're being gentlemen, right?"

Oh, if only you knew.

My cheeks immediately flush with warmth. For a moment, guilt sits heavily in the pit of my stomach. While I don't regret what's happened, I have no idea how I'm supposed to broach the subject with my brother. A small voice in the back of my head tells me I shouldn't bring it up, He really doesn't need to know. Can't a girl have a little fun from time to time? Am I not capable of making my own choices without having to report my every move?

I know I'm being selfish. These are William's friends, his former brothers at arms. I'm sure I'm stepping over several lines here, but I'm unsure how William will react. He's always been such a supportive, amazing big brother. Would he be understanding? Or will he freak out? At this point, I feel like it could go either way, but maybe it's too soon to bring it up.

I'm just having a little fun, but if I'm being perfectly honest, things are moving far faster and more seriously than I ever could have expected. There's no understanding this bond I share with the guys—including Richard, even though I know he's trying to keep me at arm's length right now. I just... *get* them. I care for each of them, Asher, Tank, Eddie, and Richard, all unique in their own ways.

It makes my head swim when I remember they're going to be leaving after the Fourth of July. Yesterday afternoon and last night were amazing, but spur of the moment. I wasn't thinking ahead to what lay in store for us. If I allow myself to get too attached, I could be setting myself up for heartbreak. I am having fun, but I have to remember this impromptu arrangement of ours is only temporary. It *will* end, and when it does, I have to be prepared to let them all go.

"They're great," I answer William eventually. "They helped me get my stuff back from Chet."

"I'm glad. He didn't give you any trouble, right?"

"No, none at all."

"Good, that's—" Somewhere in the background, I hear a voice murmur. Someone must be talking to him. "Sorry, Win. I've got to go. Very important business presentation."

I smile. "Knock 'em dead. Talk soon."

When the call ends, I take in a deep breath of fresh air, filling my lungs to the brim with the scent of pine trees and rich earth. It's so peaceful here it's easy to forget that time, does in fact, march on. Now that I'm thinking about the future, I can't stop.

How do you think you're going to make it without me?

The memory of Chet's words is all I need to kick my stubbornness up a notch. Screw him and screw my own doubt. I'm more than capable of figuring things out on my own. In fact, the prospect of starting fresh in a brand-new city excites me. New apartment, new job, new environment... The possibilities are endless. I'm sure if I spend the next few months doubling down on my freelance work— maybe I can take on a couple of new clients for smaller projects—I can squirrel away enough ahead of my move to New York.

I head back inside the lake house, refreshed and determined and filled with the promise of something new on the horizon. I think Asher, Tank, and Eddie are still in the kitchen finishing breakfast because I can hear their voices carrying down the hall, the occasional clink of utensils against plates.

Just as I pass Richard's bedroom door, I notice it's closed. On the other side, I can pick up the faint rumble of his voice through the wood.

"And you're sure it's accurate?" he asks someone. "You got this straight from his private server?"

My ears burn. As quiet as a mouse, I lean against the door and press my ear to it.

"I need you to forward everything to me," Richard says to whoever he's talking to on the phone. "This is the evidence I need. You haven't told anyone else, have you? Good." A heavy sigh. He sounds exhausted. "No, I don't have a complete plan, but I'm working on it. Just send me those emails and I'll take everything from there... Don't worry. I'll put Grey away before he has a chance to figure out it was you."

Grey?

The hairs on my arms stand on end. Is he talking about Asher?

What does he mean, put him away? I'm clearly missing something here, but it makes me sick to my stomach, nonetheless. I'm not an idiot. I've noticed things between Asher and Richard have been rocky at best. I didn't want to pry before, but if Richard plans on doing something to him... I don't know if I can look the other way.

I'm torn between going to my room, turning back to tell Asher something's up, or keeping Richard's conversation private. It'd be wrong of me to jump to conclusions. If anything, my involvement might only make things worse. Unsure what else to do, I take a step back and—

Creak.

The wooden floorboard sags beneath my weight, groaning in protest. On the other side of the door, Richard's phone call abruptly ends. I hear him shuffling, moving. I turn on my heel and head for my room, but it's too late. Richard's far too fast.

"Winona?"

I pause. "Yes?"

His dark eyes sweep over me from head to toe. "How much did you hear?"

I contemplate lying, but I see there's no point. He's caught me eavesdropping, so there's no point in denying it. Besides, I'm a terrible liar. "What evidence?" I ask. "What's going on between you and Asher, Richard?"

Richard's face hardens. "I mean this with the utmost respect, Winona, but you need to mind your own business."

"I just want to understand. Has he done something wrong?"

Instead of answering, Richard slips past me and heads for the front door. I'm hot on his trail. After years of being ignored by Chet, of being pushed aside, I refuse to accept Richard's silence. I want to be able to help them. Whatever is tearing them apart, I'm sure talking about it can't hurt.

He leaves through the front entrance, slipping into his boots quickly. When he gets outside, he practically breaks out into a full jog. I sprint full-on just to keep up with him.

"Richard, wait!"

"Leave it alone, Winona."

"Please, just talk to me."

"This has nothing to do with you."

"But it has to do with Asher, right? And Tank and Eddie? I know it does. If you won't tell me, will you at least talk to them?"

"This is something I have to do alone."

I ball my hands up into fists, storming after him as he hurriedly makes his way down a hiking trail toward the lake. "Do you feel like you can't talk to us—to me—because of what happened last night?"

"I don't know what you're talking about."

"Are you kidding?" I ask, breathless. Good God, this man needs to slow down. I can hardly keep up. "You should have seen the look on your face when you saw me with them. Are you uncomfortable with me now?"

Richard halts and turns to look at me. "I'm not uncomfortable."

"Really? Then why have you been avoiding me? Does the idea of sharing me weird you out? Do you think..." I swallow hard. "Do you think I'm awful for wanting it?"

In the blink of an eye, Richard steps forward and closes the gap between us, corralling me up against a nearby tree. He cages me in with his body, his arms stretched out with his hands balanced against the bark on either side of my head. He's close, smells too delicious for words. The darkness in his eyes is nothing short of ravenous.

"You've got it all wrong," he says, his tone dropping an octave. "I've wanted to have you since you walked in. Getting to share you with my brothers... Nothing would please me more than getting to please *you*."

"Then... Then why?"

His gaze flicks down to my lips. "I've got a lot on my plate right now. You wouldn't understand."

"I definitely won't understand if you don't tell me what's going on." I press my hands to his chest, curling my fingers in the fabric of his shirt. "You said it yourself. There's nothing wrong with asking for help. It's not a weakness."

For a moment, Richard looks stunned at my throwing his words back at him. He works his jaw, the muscles in his face tensing as he grinds his teeth. The silence feels like it lasts an eternity. I can practically hear the gears grinding inside his skull as he contemplates whether to burden me with the truth.

"We were on an assignment. Classified. I have reason to believe Asher's grandfather betrayed us and leaked our plans."

I furrow my brows. That's... definitely not what I was expecting. "But why?"

"That's the million-dollar question."

My mouth drops open, my eyes wide. "No wonder you and Asher..."

"He adamantly denies it." Richard sighs. "I don't blame him. Truly, I understand where he's coming from. I wouldn't want to blame the man who raised me, either."

"But you have proof?" I ask, my heart racing. "That's what you said on the phone, right?"

Richard nods slowly. "The colonel's private secretary, Denise. I had to call in a few favors, but she got ahold of his private correspondence. Proof he was in contact with our target ahead of the mission. I need to see it for myself and authenticate the material before I expose him."

"This sounds dangerous."

"That's why I didn't want to get you involved. If—" Richard suddenly cuts himself off, glaring at something from across the lake. I can just see it out of the corner of my eye, a bright glint of light.

"What's that?" I ask.

"Get down!" he shouts, throwing me to the forest floor just as a bullet embeds itself into the tree where the two of us were standing.

CHAPTER 13

RICHARD

"Stay low," I command, shielding Winona's body with my own. There's enough foliage to obscure us from view, but the moment we stand or try to escape, we'll no doubt be in view of the sniper stationed on the other side of the lake.

Shit, shit, shit.

A million questions run through my head. Who's shooting at us? Why are they targeting us? How did they even *find* us?

I'm certain Asher, Tank, and Eddie must have heard the gunshot, but on the off chance they didn't, I still need an exit strategy. My first and only priority is getting Winona to safety, but my options are limited. The gunman is probably already on the move, trying to find a better vantage point. If we stay put, there's a good chance we'll be killed. If we move, however, our chances of survival are just as slim. The moment we stand is the moment we give away our position. We have to haul ass or risk having our heads blown off.

Beneath me, I feel Winona trembling. She's not crying, not screaming, not freaking out, but her body betrays her mask of bravery.

"I'm going to get us out of here," I tell her hastily. "You need to do exactly as I say, alright?"

She nods, her lips pressed into a thin, worried line.

"On my mark, we're going to make a B-line back to the lake house. Stay low but keep moving."

As carefully as I can, I shrug off my jacket and ball it up in my hands, careful not to let my shoulders or arms—or more fatally, my head—peak out from behind the thick bushes obscuring us from view. I steady my breathing, my muscles tensing in preparation for what I'm about to do.

I count us down. "Three, two... *one.*"

I throw my balled-up jacket up and behind me, equal parts pleased and horrified when I hear a second shot ring out. The bullet pierces straight through the fabric like a hot knife through butter. There's no time to panic, no time to question it—only time to run.

Winona and I scramble to our feet. I take her hand and pull her along with me as we make a mad dash while the shooter is momentarily distracted. It will take them a moment to recalibrate, reload, and aim. Those few precious seconds are all that stand between death and survival.

A five-minute mile is a piece of cake for me, even on a bad day. But Winona's a civilian, untrained for this sort of pressure. Not to mention she's half my size and barely able to keep up. The lake house isn't far. I can see it just out of the corner of my eye, Tank, Asher, and Eddie are crowding onto the porch to investigate the ruckus.

"The fuck is going on?" Eddie snaps.

"Get back inside!" I hiss, still holding onto Winona's hand for dear life.

There's no space to slow down, so we barrel up the steps together and all but crash right into them and fall through the front door into the entryway. The five of us land in a pile, winded and alarmed.

"Fucking *ow*," Tank grumbles.

The first and only thing I think to do is check on Winona. I grasp her by the arms and help her sit up, looking for any signs of injury.

Apart from her black eye—which is starting to heal nicely—there isn't a scratch on her. Thank God.

"What's happening?" Asher asks.

"We were shot at!" Winona blurts out. "*Twice!*"

Looks of disbelief are shared all around, but there's no time to entertain questions.

"This location is compromised," I say, standing. "We need to move. It's only a matter of time before they try and charge the house."

"How many?" Eddie asks, climbing to his feet. He's always rip-roaring for a fight.

"I don't know," I confess, "but I'd rather not stick around to find out—"

The shattering of glass. A bullet lodged in the drywall. A decorative vase blown to bits. We're under fire. Not only are we pinned down, but none of us are armed. Our guns are locked safely in the gun safe. Even if we wanted to take our attackers on, we're at a disadvantage in every conceivable way.

"Get to the truck!" Asher shouts, quickly throwing a protective arm over Winona's shoulder to keep her low and guide her to our vehicles.

They pile into the back of my truck as I clamber into the driver's seat, hurriedly twisting the key I'd left in the ignition. The moment the engine roars to life, I throw the truck into reverse and pull out of the gravel driveway, executing a sharp three-point turn before slamming on the gas.

We're still not in the clear. One of my side-mirrors is taken out by a neatly placed bullet. Another snipes straight through the back window, the tempered glass spraying all over us. Winona screams, my men shout at me to drive faster. Only after we get around the bend and onto the main road does the chaos finally stops.

A strangely numb silence falls over us the longer we drive. It's just a matter of who wants to talk first. Naturally, my second-in-command takes charge.

"Where are we going?" Asher asks. "What was all that about? You better give us some answer, Wilder, or I swear to God—"

"I have evidence," I interject. "Hard, concrete evidence."

In the reflection of the rearview mirror, I study his expression. It's half-appalled, half-disbelieving.

"You son of a bitch," he grumbles. "How many times do I have to keep telling you the colonel—"

"Denise has obtained emails from a private server," I explain.

"His personal assistant?"

"One and the same."

In the passenger seat beside me, Tank slumps with a heavy groan. "Holy shit."

"You're sure?" Asher asks. It's rare for the man to sound so small and unsure.

"The people who were shooting at us," Eddie murmurs. "Do you think they were trying to silence us? What if Colonel Grey knows you know?"

Asher shakes his head, clearly torn. Poor bastard. "But... Why would he—"

"We need to get to Denise," I state, merging into the left lane to get ahead of a minivan going ten miles below the speed limit. We're in a hurry, and I frankly don't feel like adhering to the law. "I asked her to forward everything to me, but now I see time is of the essence. We have to get to her before the colonel does."

Tank shifts in his seat. "You don't think he'd..."

"If he knows to come after Richard," Winona whispers gravely, "then he probably knows about your informant."

The cloying silence that follows is deafening.

CHAPTER 14

WINONA

There's no time to stop, so it's a good thing Richard's gas tank is almost completely full. We drive for what feels like hours until we're well past the state border, headed all the way up to Vermont. I always enjoyed road trips as a little girl, but this, unfortunately, isn't my idea of a good time.

I've long since calmed down, my shaky hands finally steady, but it does nothing to soothe my nerves. It's been one thing after another lately. I suppose in the grand scheme of things, it could be arguably worse than being on the run. I count my lucky stars we all managed to get away unscathed.

I'm seated between Eddie and Asher in the back seat. It's chilly, the blown-out window in the back making for a terrible draft as the truck rushes toward our destination. Richard drives like a bat out of hell, weaving in and out of traffic like a madman. It's frankly a miracle we haven't been pulled over for speeding—or for the suspicious bullet holes riddling the back of the vehicle.

I must have dozed off at some point, likely the result of my inevitable adrenaline crash, because when I come to, we've arrived in a quaint little suburb complete with white picket fences, manicured lawns, and impressive bungalows with sloped roofs.

"We need to drop her off somewhere," Tank murmurs to Richard from the front seat. The truck has all but crawled to a standstill. "Does she have any relatives? Someplace safe we can leave her? If we're about to walk into another ambush—"

"Are you talking about me?" I ask, my voice groggy with sleep. I sit up a little straighter, smiling at Eddie when I notice he's been letting me rest my head against his shoulder.

Tank gives me a small smile. "Hey, sugar."

"To answer your question, no. I don't have any relatives. Well, maybe a cousin in Hawaii, but I don't know her well."

"She stays with us," Asher states firmly, "until we get to the bottom of things. I'm sure this is just a terrible misunderstanding, or..." He trails off, then adds, "Don't jump to conclusions, is what I'm saying."

Richard parks the car at the curb, right in front of a small bungalow in the middle of a cul-de-sac. There's nothing extraordinary about this place. The neighbors all look to be home, their cars parked in their driveways with a couple of lights filtering through their curtains. I hear the distant bark of a dog, the caws of birds overhead. All is calm and peaceful.

And for some reason, I'm terribly on edge.

The house in question is quiet. Maybe a little too quiet.

"Wait in the car," Richard says. The guys all move to get out, and I realize he's talking to me.

"I want to come with you," I insist. For added measure, "I'll be safer with the four of you than if you leave me in here alone."

Eddie snorts, shooting Richard a smug grin. "The woman has a point."

Richard sighs. "Stay close."

It's all the permission I need.

We approach the house together. So far, there's nothing out of the ordinary. On the surface, it's your typical suburban home. I pay close attention to the begonia flowers growing in the garden, as well as the water sprinkler set on a timer. I know I'm out of my element here, that this cloak and dagger and danger really isn't a place for a little editor like me, but my gift for attention to detail is proving useful. I can see the little things—minor clues the guys otherwise ignore.

Like the faint outline of a muddy footprint on the welcome mat. Size fifteen double wide, a heavy-duty boot by the looks of the tread. Unless Denise is as large as Tank, these footprints don't belong to her. I tap Richard's shoulder and point at the print. He nods in understanding, holding his finger up to his lips before looking to his brothers. He signals with his hand, *slow*.

He reaches for the handle. The front door is unlocked.

Inside, we hear the muffled cry of a woman.

They move like lightning, so incredibly organized and coordinated. Richard charges in first, followed by Tank, then Asher, and then Eddie, with me following in the rear.

I'm alarmed to find the house in a complete state of destruction. The coffee table is overturned, there's broken glass on the floor, and several dents in the walls. Picture frames are knocked loose while cushion stuffing litters the ground.

"Someone, help me!" a woman shrieks.

The guys barrel down the hall together toward what I can only assume is Denise's room. I stand back, alarmed when I see a man dressed in all black with his arm wrapped around the woman's throat. He has a gun to her head. All it would take is a quick squeeze of the trigger.

But Richard doesn't let it get that far. He lunges, throwing his full body weight at the assailant. They both slam to the floor, the gun clattering onto the tile. Tank kicks the weapon away while Asher and Eddie gang up on the attacker. Without thinking, I help, too, reaching for Denise.

I wrap my arms around her and guide her away from the chaos. She cries, her earsplitting wails just as loud as the men fighting to rescue her.

"It's okay," I say as calmly as I can manage. "You're safe now. We've got you."

"He was going to—I don't know where he came from—Oh my God, he was trying to—" Denise sobs so violently I'm scared she might pass out, so I hold her a little tighter.

"Don't let him get away!" Eddie bellows.

Asher grunts like he's taken a hit. "Fuck, wait—"

A window breaks. I hear huffing and puffing, along with a sharp *well, fuck* from Tank. It isn't long before the guys vacate the room to find Denise and me.

"Are you alright?" Richard asks her.

Denise glares at him, her bloodshot eyes practically popping out of their sockets. "Are you out of your mind? Do I *look* like I'm alright?" She rubs her throat, gasps for breath. "Did you get him?"

"He got away," Eddie growls.

The poor woman looks like she's two seconds away from fainting. "Got away? How could he have gotten—"

I see it before anyone else does. The front of Asher's shirt is completely soaked in red. The fabric has been sliced clean through, exposing the deep gash trailing across his stomach and upper hip.

"Asher!" I gasp, stepping toward him. "Oh my God, we need to get you to a hospital."

"I'm fine," he grumbles, pressing his palm against the wound to slow the bleeding. "I'll live."

"This isn't the time to act tough, dammit!"

"No, he's right," Richard says. "He'll live. It's not that deep. What's important right now is that Denise hands over the emails. You *do* have the emails, right?"

Denise combs a shaky hand through her hair. "Uh... Yeah, I... They're on my laptop."

"Bring it with you," he continues. "We can't stay here. There's a good chance our friend will return with backup to finish the job."

My skin burns, every sensation heightened with fear. What the hell is going on? Is this what an out-of-body experience feels like?

Everything is off kilter, like I'm two inches from where my body actually is, watching everything as it happens as though I'm not really here. I'm standing on the sharp edge of a razer, waiting to either fall or be sliced clean in half by powers out of my control.

"I need..." Denise grasps at her chest, struggling. "I need to pack."

"There's no time," Richard snaps.

I rub a small circle against Denise's back and give Richard an exasperated look. "Give her a chance to breathe. She's in shock."

"Wilder is right," Tank says, his tone sympathetic. "Tell us what to grab. And please tell me you have a first aid kit for Asher."

Denise nods, her whole body trembling uncontrollably as tears stain her cheeks. "My laptop's in my bedroom," she manages to rasp. "That's what the man kept asking me for. The colonel's private emails are on there. And... And there should be a basic first aid kit under the sink in my bathroom."

"We move out in two minutes," Richard orders.

Everyone gets moving. Our survival depends on our swiftness.

I'm just about to guide Denise out to the car, but Eddie stops me. "There's not enough room. We need a bigger ride."

I turn to Denise, taking her hands to give her fingers a light squeeze. "What kind of car do you have?"

She chews on the inside of her cheek. "A minivan. Nothing stylish."

"We're not going for flashy," Richard says sternly. "A minivan will do perfectly."

CHAPTER 15

ASHER

The motel we find on the edge of town is...well, it's not the Ritz.
I'm in the bathroom, seated awkwardly on the edge of the small porcelain tub as I stitch myself up. I should have seen the knife sooner, should have known not to let my guard down. This is what I get for being distracted—but honestly, who can blame me? If my grandfather is guilty of sending the sniper and the man who attacked his own personal assistant...

I shake my head, like it might help shake loose the thoughts that have been plaguing me. I'm still in denial. I can't believe any of this. I don't *want* to believe any of this.

The sink has been running hot water for over twenty minutes, the steam fogging up the bathroom mirror. I'm no field medic, but I know enough basic first aid that I can manage my own stitches. I've done my best to sanitize everything—cleaning the wound thoroughly and dipping the sewing needle in a small cup of vodka from the motel room's bar—but this place is so dingy I'm a little worried I might give myself a staph infection from staring at the floor for too long.

A soft knock sounds at the door. I know it's Winona even before she calls out, "Are you doing okay in there?" She lets herself in. I don't miss her small sigh of relief when she sees I haven't bled out and died.

"I'm okay, angel. Don't worry about me."

Instead of turning away, she steps into the small bathroom space and picks up a clean wash towel from off the bathroom counter. She runs it under the stream of hot water, rings it out, and dutifully kneels before me. I've finished with my stitches, but there's still a trace amount of blood. Winona must not be squeamish, because she gently brings the cloth to my wound and wipes up what she can in gentle dabbing motions.

"You don't have to do this," I murmur. I sound exhausted and bitter. I *am* exhausted and bitter.

Winona shushes me, totally focused on the task at hand. I appreciate the coolness of her fingers and the obvious care behind her touch. It doesn't hurt in the slightest, which is a surprise.

"You're pretty good at this," I say.

She smiles softly. "I used to patch William up all the time."

"Is that so?"

"He got into a lot of fights when he was in school," she says, her eyes distant and far away. "He'd come home all banged up. He was angry all the time, especially after Mom and Dad died. He had nowhere to take out all that aggression. He calmed down a lot once he joined the Marines. I think it helped him, having a direction and purpose in life."

I reach out and tuck a few strands of her hair behind her ear. I just can't help myself. Like a soothing action, not dissimilar to the way a child sucks on his thumb or when people chew on their nails. Playing with Winona's silky hair puts me in a better mood, helps me find peace.

"William never talked much about your parents," I admit. "He was always very private about it."

Winona shrugs her shoulder. "I couldn't have been more than four, so I don't really remember. William was fourteen. Car accident.

We lived with our aunt and uncle after they died. But they're gone now too."

She speaks so clinically about it, her lines rehearsed and devoid of any real emotion. In some ways, I think that makes sense. It's as she said—she doesn't really remember.

Which makes my heart ache for her.

"I lost my parents in a car accident, too," I murmur.

Winona peers up at me, her long lashes fluttering as she blinks. "I'm sorry to hear that. How old were you?"

"Probably five. Not much older than you, really. My grandfather took me in."

I don't know what to make of the look she gives me. It's pity and understanding and concern all mixed into one. It's a unique feeling, losing one's parents at such a young age. Most people assume I must have been lonely growing up, missing them. But the truth of the matter is I didn't. Not really. Because how are you supposed to miss people you never truly knew?

"What's he like, your grandfather?"

Winona's question surprises me. Given everything that's going on, I'm not too sure what to tell her. If I place myself in her shoes, I can easily understand why my friends think of him as some sort of monster. A traitor. The villain.

But that's not Gramps. George has always been there for me, my savior who took me in when I had nowhere else to turn to.

"Strict," I answer, "but always fair. He never showed his affection physically. Hugs and kisses were definitely not his thing. But he liked to show it in other ways."

"Like what?"

I smile to myself. "Gramps likes to go on fishing trips. When I'd ace a test or win a basketball game, he'd find the time to take me fishing. Just the two of us, out on the lake in a canoe, fishing from sunup 'til sundown. And the whole time, he'd spend it telling me his old war stories. The battles he fought, the people he saved, and the brothers he met along the way."

There's a sparkle in Winona's eyes, her smile stretching across her lips. "He must have had some great tales to share."

"I drank them up," I confess. "I couldn't get enough."

"Is he one of the reasons you joined the Marines?"

"More or less. I think... I just wanted to make Gramps proud. Naturally, I thought the way to do that was to follow in his footsteps, but now..." I trail off, unable to finish my thought. "My grandfather is a good man," I insist. "I swear, Winona. Whatever these emails are, whatever proof Richard thinks he's found... There has to be some sort of explanation."

Winona rests her hands on my knees and tilts her chin up. She hesitates for a moment, but eventually says, "I have a question for you, and I want you to answer honestly. Can you do that for me, Asher?"

I swallow hard, my throat unbearably dry. There's nothing but the rush of water to listen to, along with the hard thuds of my heart in my chest. I lick my lips and nod slowly. "What is it, angel?"

"*If*—and I'm saying *if*—it really is the colonel behind these attacks... Are you willing to accept it?"

Her question leaves me hollow, cold, and empty. Am I willing to accept that my grandfather not only sold us out to the enemy, but sold out *his own grandson*? Evidence and hypotheticals be damned, who in their right mind can take that information in stride? It makes me want to scream. What a cruel twist of fate, pitting me against the only family I have left in the world.

I have too many unanswered questions. The feeling in my gut tells me there has to be more to this story. Maybe Gramps is being framed. The man who raised me and the man who betrayed me... They don't line up. I can't adjust to this dissonance, this misalignment. Something bigger is going on here, but there's no way I'm getting to the bottom of things while cooped up in this dingy motel bathroom.

I need answers, and there's only one person who can give them to me.

"Yes," I lie to her. It doesn't feel good.

Winona's smile is so sweet and trusting it breaks me in two. But I have to protect her, and this is the only way I know how. I refuse to see her caught in the crossfire, trapped in a situation that has literally nothing to do with her. Until I can figure out what's going on, I need to keep her out of harm's way.

Slowly, I lean forward and press my lips to hers, kissing her as tenderly as I can manage. It takes every ounce of my willpower not to devour her mouth. Everything about Winona ignites a firestorm within me. Having her isn't enough. I need to claim her. She brings out something animalistic in me, something feral, and I'll be damned if I try and stop it.

Winona moans into our kiss, her voice vibrating through me. The scent of roses and peaches engulfs me, leaving me with a contact high. I know things are moving really fast. Maybe a little *too* fast. But I'm convinced this woman really must come from on high, because there's truly no way to explain the hold she has over my body and soul.

"Angel, I—"

Three sharp knocks sound at the door. Tank steps in, looking a tad agitated. "Denise pulled up the emails," he says. "You're going to want to see this."

Dread claws through me. I really *don't* want to see this, but I stand up anyway. Winona quickly helps apply a fresh bandage to protect my stitches and rubs my arm in a comforting manner. There's no sense in putting this off any longer.

Everyone else is gathered near the motel room's provided table. It's small, cramped, and leaning to one side, but it's just enough space for Denise to set up shop. Her laptop is open, screen blindingly bright, several emails pulled up for all to see.

I gauge my brothers' reactions.

Tank looks miserable.

Eddie looks shell-shocked.

And Richard looks like he wants to fly off the handle.

"This is it," Denise mutters, her voice hoarse from all her crying. "As his personal assistant, I normally have access to all his correspondence. Mail, telephone, email. It's all done on an approved server. We can't have sensitive information floating around or getting lost in someone's spam folder."

I bite my tongue. *Hard.* "Then how did you know about the private server?"

Denise takes a deep breath, casting a glance of suspicion in my direction. "I'd noticed Colonel Grey acting... strange lately. Always on his phone, taking unscheduled calls. So I did some digging. I thought it was my fault at first. Figured maybe I'd forgotten to adjust his calendar or missed an important message from a superior officer. And then I found these."

I hover behind her, staring at the laptop screen. What I see next is almost enough to kill me where I stand.

Maps, schedules, direct coordinates. Movement patterns, formations, detailed dossiers for every member of our confidential strike force—myself included. Our ranks, information on our families, our medical histories. Everything under the sun is contained in these emails.

"There's no signature," I point out.

Eddie huffs. "So?"

I shake my head. "You have no proof the colonel wrote these himself."

Richard crosses his arm over his chest. "You've got to be fucking kidding me, Grey."

My nostrils flare. Everything aches. "For all you know, someone could have drafted and sent these on his computer and made it *look* like he was the one who sent them. I'm assuming the email address is encrypted?"

Denise nods, clears her throat. "Well, yes, but—"

"And did you ever *see* him send these emails?"

"Well, no—"

"Then you're accusing my grandfather of treason based on

circumstantial evidence!" Anger boils deep within my veins, so hot and painful I almost can't see straight.

"Easy," Tank warns. "Take a deep breath. You need to calm down, Asher."

"Don't tell me to calm down—"

My phone rings loudly, cutting through the tension in the room. When I pull it out of my pocket, I stare at the caller ID on screen.

"Well?" Winona asks.

I grit my teeth. "It's him. He's FaceTiming."

Richard's nostrils flare. "Answer it."

CHAPTER 16

WINONA

When Asher answers the call, I'm genuinely surprised by what I see. Colonel George Grey is nothing like I thought he'd be. He doesn't look like the villain Richard makes him out to be, but he certainly doesn't strike me as the wholesome grandfather-figure Asher described either. The colonel is somewhere in the middle, existing between the two extremes.

He has a hard, stern face made ten times more severe by his scowl. But his body is soft, his round belly and double chin giving him less of an intimidating air. I can definitely see the familial resemblance. Asher shares the same nose and eyes, except—

Except the colonel's eyes are dead. Close to it, at least. They lack any semblance of warmth, two black voids where light goes to die. Combined with his sweet, almost disarming smile, the colonel is nothing short of jarring. I'm torn between fearing the man and giving him the benefit of the doubt. Never in my life have I met such a walking contradiction, and he hasn't spoken yet.

"Asher, my boy," the colonel greets. His smile is friendly, but his tone is anything but. There's an irritated edge to his words. "And hello to your friends. I see Denise is there with you, as well."

The air in the room shifts, heavy and uncomfortable.

Asher speaks first. "Gramps, did you send those men after us?"

"What do you mean?"

Behind me, Richard clenches his fists. "Don't play dumb, Colonel. We were attacked."

The colonel's face darkens. "How terrible."

Out of the corner of my eye, I can see how agitated Eddie is getting. He shifts his weight from foot to foot, grinding his teeth so hard I can hear them squeak. "What's your game?" he seethes. "We have your fucking emails. We *know*."

A shiver runs down my spine, goosebumps breaking over my arms and the back of my neck. My stomach churns, a massive wave of nausea hitting me when I see the colonel's large, slow smile. It's chilling. Inhuman.

"I understand you're upset," he says calmly.

"Upset?" Tank huffs. "That's the understatement of the year."

"This is what's going to happen," the colonel continues without so much as a blink. "Denise, you're going to destroy any copies you have. We can all forget this ever happened. Wipe our hands clean of this nonsense, and we can all move on."

Richard shakes his head. "Why the fuck would we do that? You're a traitor to your country. You sold out your own *grandson*. We're going to make sure you're held accountable."

Once again, the colonel doesn't look like he gives two fucks. With a simple shrug, he turns the camera on his phone to reveal someone. My eyes widen when I see who it is, my heart plummeting into the pit of my stomach. Tears sting my eyes.

"William?" I screech.

My big brother is tied to a chair. I can't get a sense of the room they're in, but it's dark and impossible to place. William's hands are bound behind his back, his ankles strapped to the legs of his chair with thick black zip ties. I count my lucky stars he doesn't appear harmed in any way, but in the grand scheme of things, it's not exactly a comfort.

"Let him go!" I scream. "He has nothing to do with this."

"Oh, you must be the little sister. I read up about you."

I think I'm going to throw up. I've never known terror quite like this. What does the colonel know? How can he use that information to his advantage? I feel violated, like something insidious has crawled beneath my skin.

"Please," I mumble. "Please, let William go. What could you possibly want with him?"

"It's called leverage, my dear. I always have a contingency in place. When the four of you returned from your mission, I knew I had to cover my bases."

"But why?" Eddie snaps.

"My motivations are none of your concern," the colonel says coldly. "I've been tracking William Wren for some time. He used to be a part of your platoon, after all. When I heard he was in Seattle, I reached out pretending to be an investor."

I ball my fists up so tight I swear my nails break through the skin of my palms. I'm outraged on my brother's behalf. How dare the colonel trick him. But no matter how badly I want to lose it, to cuss the bastard out, his threat comes through loud and clear. If we don't do as he says, if we make him more upset than he already is—

He's going to kill my brother.

"Destroy those emails," the colonel says.

Richard steps forward. "No."

I grip his arm, giving his bicep a firm squeeze as I cast him with a pleading look. "Richard, there has to be *something* we can do."

"We don't negotiate with terrorists. Period."

The colonel clicks his tongue. "Are you really willing to sacrifice your brother at arms? How disappointing. Your steadfastness has always been your greatest strength and your greatest weakness, Wilder."

My throat closes up. I can't breathe. "Don't hurt my brother. Please, I'm begging you."

"You want him alive? Then do as I ask and destroy those emails. I won't ask again."

I'm two seconds from having a nervous breakdown. I understand why Richard won't cave in, but I can't risk anything happening to William, either. He's the only family I have left. I'm caught between a rock and a hard place.

Asher, who's been largely silent up until this point, finally says, "We need time to think." I've never heard him sound so small before. On one hand, I want to reach out and comfort him. But on the other...

The colonel chuckles almost good-naturedly. "Very well, dear boy. If you think that'll help. Just know this: if you try anything, I *will* put a bullet between his eyes. You have until the end of the week to make your decision."

The call ends.

I'm absolutely gutted.

The yelling back and forth is endless. We're no closer to a solution than we were an hour ago.

"We can't let him get away with this," Richard insists. "I say we forward the evidence to as many outlets as we can. Once the media catches wind of his double-cross, he'll be done for."

"And risk Wren's life?" Tank argues. "It's obvious the fucker has no problem going after loose ends. He tried with you and Winona. He tried with Denise. There's no doubt in my mind he'll kill William out of sheer spite if we don't do as he says.

"What's to stop him from doing something like this again?" Eddie grumbles. "Hell, maybe he has, and we've been none the wiser. This might be our only chance to expose him."

I've heard enough. My nerves are shot and I want nothing more than a breath of fresh air. Quietly, I slip away from the group and head for the door, stepping out into the chilly evening.

I don't think we were followed, so I'm not uncomfortable being out in the open. The landscape is bare, and there are no signs of anyone suspicious. We're on the ground floor of this seedy place, so I plop down on the curb and stare out into the parking lot, numb as can be.

I'm out of my depth here. What was supposed to be a month of lying low has now turned into a never-ending nightmare, constantly spiraling out of control. None of it feels real. Hell, I was talking to William on the phone just this morning. How did things tailspin so quickly? At what point did the colonel capture my brother? He said he needed a contingency plan... Does this mean if his sniper had managed to kill Richard, William would have been left unharmed?

I rake my fingers through my hair and exhale slowly. The last thing I want is for anyone to get hurt. Asher, Tank, Eddie, Richard, Denise, my brother... none of them deserve this. What the colonel is doing to them is just so *cruel*—and we don't even know his reasoning behind it. Whatever the case may be, it doesn't change the fact that my brother's life hinges on the guys' decision.

I'm so lost in thought I don't realize Tank has exited the motel room to join me on the curb until he's seated next to me, our knees knocking together as he presses his good arm against mine.

"Are you okay, sugar?" he asks softly.

I shake my head. There's no sense in lying. "Fuck no."

"We're going to figure this out," he promises. "I swear it, Winona."

"But *how*? No matter what you guys choose to do, we lose regardless."

Tank presses his lips into a thin line as he slides his arm over my shoulders. He pulls me in, the warmth of his body soaking into mine. His presence brings me immediate comfort. "Listen to me well—we're *not* going to lose."

"But William—"

"I know you're worried about him because he's your brother, but don't forget he was once one of us. One of the finest Marines I ever had the honor of serving with. William's as tough as nails. He's going to be fine, and so are we."

I peer at him. "Tell me there's something I can do to help."

"Winona..."

"*Please*, Tank. I can be useful. Just... tell me what to do, and I'll do it. Whatever it takes to save my brother and put the colonel away."

Tank's expression softens as he leans in, capturing my lips with a sweet kiss. "Now that you mention it, there *is* something you can do."

"Tell me."

"You can come with me to my family's farm in Alabama."

I frown in confusion. "Your family's farm? Why?"

"We need somewhere where we can lie low. Returning to the lake house isn't an option, and since you have no relatives, we can't just drop you off. Denise is going to fly to London, Ontario, to stay with her sister. She should be safe there."

I chew on the inside of my cheek. "You... want to get rid of me?"

"No, sugar. We're not getting rid of you. But things are probably going to get dangerous."

"It's *already* dangerous."

"That's why we won't have you in harm's way."

"But my brother—"

"You leave William to us," Tank says sternly. "We'll rescue him. But we can't do that if we're constantly having to worry about you."

I sit up a little straighter. "You make me sound like a burden."

"That's not what I mean, Winona. You're not a burden. We just... care about you deeply, is all. I can't speak on behalf of the guys, but I'd be beside myself if anything happened to you."

"So you're hiding me away?"

"To keep you safe," Tank insists. The emotion in his voice is so powerful it makes my throat close. "To protect you, Winona. That's all I want. If the colonel is willing to stoop as low as keeping William hostage, who's to say he won't try to come after you, too?"

I believe him when he says this. We've only known each other for a short time, but I can say with the utmost confidence that Tank is as honest as they come. He's open and he's caring and he's fun. At the end of the day, I think I'd trust him with my life again and again without question.

And maybe taking me to his family's farm isn't such a bad thing. I'm out of my element here. I'm genuinely concerned I'd end up getting in the way. While my heart is in the right place, I shouldn't fool myself into thinking I have the expertise to go up against someone as cunning and conniving as the colonel.

"Okay," I murmur against Tank's lips. "Hide me away, Tank. Keep me safe."

"With my life, Winona."

CHAPTER 17

TANK

After we drop Denise off at the airport and ensure she gets through the gates, we immediately hit the road. It will take us roughly fourteen hours or so—maybe thirteen if I gun it—to get to the Quill family farm just outside of Florence, Alabama, and I can tell the others are just as antsy as I am to get going. Staying in one place too long can't possibly bode well for us.

Denise's minivan might not be the flashiest ride from here to Tennessee, but it's got great gas mileage. We only have to stop twice to fill up, each an opportunity to stretch our weary legs. We never dawdle, though. Time is of the essence. It's as the colonel said—we have until the end of the week to make our decision; otherwise, it's lights out for William.

Something tells me it'll be lights out, regardless, but I wouldn't dare say it aloud. I can see how upset Winona is already, and I'd rather not run my mouth and stress her out further.

Asher hasn't said a damn thing in hours.

He sits beside me in the passenger seat, staring ahead blankly at the road stretched out before us. I've known the man for many years, and I've never seen him more quiet and sullen. It's jarring, really.

Asher's normally always in good spirits. He's the optimist of our little brotherhood, the guy who always tries to see the glass half-full. And now he's a ghost of himself. Utterly distraught and destroyed by the revelation that his own grandfather, a man he holds in the highest regard, does in fact have a darker side.

When I see the big wooden sign arching over the front entrance of the Quill family farm, I nearly jump for joy—and if it weren't for the seatbelt, I probably would have. I haven't been home to see Nana in so long. I only wish the reason for my return wasn't so dire.

I pull the minivan up to the main house, a large wooden lodge that's been renovated several times throughout the decades. It once belonged to my grandfather, and my grandfather's father. This place was built sturdy—just like every single one of the Quill men.

Nana practically bursts through the screen door and onto the porch when she hears the car pull up. She holds her cane over her head, waving it like she's trying to signal a fighter jet in for landing.

"There's my boy!" she squeals, barreling toward me the second I get out from behind the driver's seat. Nana might be pushing eighty, but she's as squirrely as the day she was born. The little woman practically flings herself at me, and I catch her with ease.

"Hi, Nana! It's so good to see you."

She knocks me alongside the head with her cane's handle. "What's taken you so long? Don't you know I'm getting old? You need to visit me more often. One of these days I'm gonna croak, and you're sure as hell gonna regret it."

I laugh. "I'm sorry, Nana. You know me, always busy." I gesture behind me. "You remember the boys, don't you?"

"Why, of course! Haven't you boys been eating? I swear, y'all get skinnier every time you come to visit."

Richard manages a polite nod. I know he doesn't feel like being courteous, but I'm grateful he can at least keep up the pretense where Nana's concerned. "A pleasure seeing you again, ma'am. And we eat just fine."

Nana's eyes finally flit down to my slinged arm. "Good Heavens, what on Earth happened to you, boy?"

"It's a long story."

"Is this the reason you called out of the blue asking for a place to stay? You know you don't actually have to call, right? Just pop on in and—" Nana glances around the group again, noticing Winona, who's just now getting out of the car. "Well, I'll be. Aren't you going to introduce me to the pretty lady, Joseph?"

I chuckle. Nana's the only one who ever calls me by my first name, but she always says it like a tease. "Nana, this is Winona Wren. Winona, this is my grandmother, Geraldine Quill."

Winona smiles sweetly, but there's no hiding the exhaustion in her eyes. "It's nice to meet you."

My grandmother shakes her hand, squinting at Winona suspiciously. "A call out of the blue. A sudden visit. And a pretty lady in the back of your car... Tank, you didn't get this poor thing pregnant, did you?"

I nearly choke on my tongue. "Nana!"

Behind me, Eddie snorts, trying and failing to hide his amusement.

Nana waves me off. "I'm just checking. Can't blame me for hoping."

"Nana!"

"Come inside, all of you. Is anyone hungry? I can whip up a little something if you're feeling puckish. I really don't mind."

"If it's alright," Winona says softly, "would I be able to lay down for a bit?"

"Of course, of course! You must be exhausted after such a long drive. Here, let me show you to your room. How long did you say you were staying again, Joseph?"

I glance at the others. Asher can't meet my eyes, Eddie shrugs, and Richard has his walls up. Our call with the colonel has shaken our team to the core.

"A week, more or less," I answer.

"Plenty of time for us to catch up," Nana says chipperly. "Come along, dear, this way."

It's almost surreal being back in my childhood home after all this time. Everything's the same, yet nothing *feels* the same. I'm a different man from the one who left all those years ago. I'm older, stronger... maybe a little more beaten down. In a world of endless chaos, it's nice to come back to the smell of Nana's cooking and the warmth of the crackling fireplace.

While Nana guides Winona upstairs, Richard claps a hand onto my good shoulder. "She'll be safe here?" he asks me under his breath.

"I know this place doesn't look like much, but it's basically a covert fortress. The fences are electric. The main house is on top of a hill, so we'll be able to see people coming and going from the road no problem. Not to mention Nana's packing. She's been known to sit on her porch with a shotgun to shoot warning shots at trespassers. There's no way anyone's getting to Winona here."

Richard nods. "Good."

"I think I'm going to skip dinner and go to bed, too," Asher mutters, barely audible despite the fact he's standing only two feet away. His eyes are cast to the floor, his shoulders slumped.

"I might hit the sack, too," Eddie mumbles.

"We'll reconvene in the morning," Richard says. "I've had enough of talking ourselves in circles."

He has a point. Right now, we only have two options, neither of which is appealing. Unless something in the status quo shifts, we might be stuck choosing between saving William's life and turning in a corrupt Marine. My guts tie up in impossible knots.

There's no winning, no matter what we do.

I rise with the sun, the pale-yellow beams of light streaming in through the sheer curtains of my childhood bedroom. It's nice, waking up to the sound of barnyard animals and the whinny of horses out in the pasture. I guess being back has reawakened the farmer in me, because I immediately rise when I hear the call of the rooster outside.

With a wide yawn, I slip out from under the covers and throw my legs over the edge of the bed. It's smaller than I remember. Or maybe the problem is I've grown too large for it.

Slowly, I make my way to the window to take in the farm, the floorboards creaking under my weight. I'm surprised when I see Winona standing by the chicken coop, watching as the hens and their chicks wander around, pecking at the grass beneath their feet. Curiosity burns in the pit of my stomach. It can't be earlier than six. What's Winona doing up and out all by her lonesome?

I'm going to have to fix that.

Mid-June in Alabama means humidity and heat, but because it's early, there's a nice little breeze. Winona's shivering when I reach her, so I instinctually shrug off my jacket and slip it over her shoulders, wondering if the shiver is because of all that's happened.

She gasps softly, surprised by my appearance. "O-oh, thank you, Tank."

"My pleasure, sugar."

The dark circles beneath her eyes are cause for concern, are the edges of her eyes, which are red-rimmed and puffy. The thought of Winona crying the entire night doesn't sit well with me. In fact, it hurts. Like her pain is my pain—and I want nothing more than to make it all go away.

I wrap an arm around her lower back and lean against the fencing with her to observe the chickens. "Did you not sleep?" I whisper.

"How could I?" she asks around a bitter laugh. "Some madman has my brother hostage and there isn't a damn thing I can do about it. Have you and the guys—"

I shake my head, sensing her question before she finishes. "We haven't made a decision yet."

Winona deflates, shrinking in on herself. "I see."

I can't bear to see her like this, so I do the only thing that comes to mind. I lean in and press a tender kiss to her cheek, her temple, to her hair. I hold her as tight as I'm able, every kiss an attempt at bringing her some small semblance of comfort. We're in the same boat, she and I. I want William to come back alive, too.

"Tank," she murmurs, turning to face me. She presses her hands against my chest as I continue to pepper her face with sweet kisses. Eventually, her fingers climb up to curl in my hair. "Tank, *kiss* me."

I do so, unable to deny her a thing.

Our lips slot together easily, a perfect fit. She tastes sweeter than honey, feels softer than a cloud. I curse my rotten luck that we couldn't have met under better circumstances. Seeing Winona in this much pain infuriates me. She deserves better. I'd move Heaven and Earth if it meant I could see Winona smile—*really* smile—without a single care in the world.

One thing leads to another. Our kiss deepens, my tongue sliding over hers. Winona moans as she combs her fingers through my hair. I roll my hips against her, my stiffening erection searching for the warmth of her thighs. When she pulls away, I see nothing but hunger. I know without a shadow of a doubt that I have to have her, here and now.

"Come with me," I say, taking her hand.

"Where are we going?"

I tilt my chin toward the old barn just a few yards away where we store all the hay. "Let me take your worries away, sugar."

"Do you think we should..."

"What is it?"

"Should we let the guys know?"

"Not this time. I want you all to myself today."

CHAPTER 18

WINONA

I t's so nice and cozy here. The sweet smell of straw and wood fills me with a sense of calm. Tank takes his jacket back and spreads it out over a soft mound of hay, inviting me to lie down with him as we continue to kiss feverishly in the early morning light.

My hands move of their own accord, exploring the wide expanse of his chest and shoulders. It still isn't enough, though. I need to feel him on me, inside me, everywhere contact is possible. My skin is incendiary, a wildfire out of control. My brain no longer subscribes to logic or reason, only an all-consuming need to make this man mine.

Without thinking, I hook my leg over his hip and use the momentum to pin Tank on his back. I feel powerful like this, trapping this big mountain of a man between my thighs. The heat of his hard cock against my core sends a delightful shiver racing up and down my spine. I earn a low, fierce growl from him when I roll my hips, grinding at a leisurely pace. I love how he moves with me, one hand on my hip to provide me balance while he thrusts his hips up to meet my every motion.

"Winona..."

I love the way he says my name. So much reverence and awe, like he's saying a prayer. I want to bask in his adoration forever, but we only have so much time.

"I want to ride you," I murmur. "I want to make you feel good, Tank."

He hums, his meaty fingers digging into my sides. "Go on, sugar. Show me what you got."

I'm convinced my hands are completely autonomous at this point, because they move with such speed and precision my mind can't possibly be giving them orders. I'm quick to disrobe and quicker still to help Tank out of the confines of his pants. His impressive length stands up in greeting, red and throbbing with want.

A slow, low moan escapes me as I sink onto him, relishing the slight burn of the stretch. Pleasure consumes me. I'm suddenly so full my body trembles, the air knocked straight out of my lungs.

I'm liberated when I'm with him. With all of them, really. For this brief moment in time, I can forget about the outside world and all the terrible things happening. Instead of stewing in my worry, in my inability to help, I can lose myself in the sensation of Tank's body and the way he expertly thumbs at my clit and how he has me hurtling over the edge of climax before I have the chance to realize what's even happened.

"Such a good girl," he moans, throbbing inside me. "I can't get enough of you."

"Tell me it's going to be okay," I rasp. "Tell me it's all going to be okay."

Tank pulls me in close and presses his lips to mine. "You ain't got nothing to worry about. Not as long as you've got us."

Us.

Not *me*, but *us*. The idea of being shared with four wonderful, sexy, infuriatingly handsome men is going to take some getting used to. Especially because it no longer feels like a temporary summer fling. Things have gotten so serious, both between us and the circumstances in which we find ourselves. I have a hard time picturing going our separate ways.

I'm sure there's a good handful of people who might tell me I'm in over my head. That I'm crazy for even entertaining the thought—but I don't care. Screw the judgment, screw the shame. I'm doing what makes me feel good, and I won't listen to anyone who tells me otherwise.

It only takes a few more upward thrusts for Tank to come tumbling after me. My core throbs around his cock, clenching his shaft tightly as we breathe heavily through our mutual ecstasy. One thing I've noticed about Tank is that he likes to bring my hand up to his face, kissing my palm and gently pressing my fingers against his cheek. The more I think about it, the guys all have their own way of showing their affection.

Tank seems to like my hands on him. Asher loves to play with my hair. With Eddie, it's deep, unbreakable eye contact—so intense and addicting I'm convinced we're the only two souls alive. And Richard...

Well, I don't really know about Richard. Yet. Back at the lake house, I was still filled with the hope that maybe something could happen between us. He admitted he thought of me, *wanted* me. But then the shooting happened, shattering the fragile possibility that maybe I'd get to have him, too.

"We should head back inside," Tank murmurs against the inside of my wrist. "I'm sure the others will wonder where you've gone."

I nod, still a little breathless. I'm sure I look like a wild mess, but I'm not embarrassed.

We get redressed quickly. Tank plucks a few loose pieces of straw from my hair with a chuckle. It's a quick walk out of the barn and toward the main house, but where I was expecting the smell of breakfast and the sound of quiet morning conversation, all I hear is—

"Fuck you, Richard!" Asher growls, venom dripping off his every word.

"No, fuck *you*," Richard growls right back.

I hurry into the house, scurrying into the living room area. I'm alarmed to find Asher and Richard in each other's faces, their body language tense and threatening with explosive force. Eddie stands between them, trying to play peacekeeper with both his hands outstretched. He may be acting as a barrier, but Asher and Richard are loaded shotguns, ready to go off at a moment's notice—regardless of who might be caught in the crossfire.

"What's going on?" I ask.

Richard looks caught out, while Asher is nothing short of pissed.

"He wants to take matters into his own hands," Asher seethes. "He wants to take out the colonel."

"We've handled missions that were far riskier," Richard argues. "If we can get to the colonel before he has a chance to hurt William—"

"You're talking about killing a superior officer. Forget he's my grandfather for a second, you're talking about killing one of our own!"

"One of our own?" Richard yells, incredulous. "He's made it perfectly clear he's no longer on our side."

"Let me at least talk to him."

"He waived the right to talk the moment he sold us out."

"I can get through to him," Asher insists. "Let me see him, and—"

"And what?"

"I'll negotiate for William's release."

"You know as well as I do there's no way he'll do that. We know too much. *All* of us." Richard's eyes flit over and land on me. He's normally too distant for me to get a read on, but there's no denying the concern in his eyes. "The colonel is going to kill every single one of us. That's the only way he can make this go away."

Asher runs a hand through his hair, sighing in exasperation. "I don't believe that."

"You don't *want* to believe it," Eddie grumbles.

"Shut the fuck up, Luna."

"But he's right," Tank interjects, his voice calm. "You're biased, Asher. You shouldn't be making any decisions where the colonel is concerned."

Richard's chest puffs out. "You need to stand down, Grey."

Asher's hands curl into tight fists. "Don't fucking tell me to stand down, Wilder."

My heart twists painfully in my chest. I can't stand by any longer and watch as they tear themselves apart. I step forward, anxiously grasping Richard's arm. "Stop it, both of you!"

Eddie shoots me a warning look. "Careful, Winona—"

"Don't you see what's happening?" I cry. "If you're too busy fighting each other, the colonel *wins*."

"Stay out of this," Asher grumbles. "This has nothing to do with you."

"Like hell it doesn't! He has my brother!"

Richard ignores me, his eyes locked onto Asher like a homing beacon. "We're going to do this my way, or else—"

"Or else what?" Asher snaps back, interrupting.

There's some pushing, some shoving.

"Would you two *relax*?" Eddie hisses, pushing back.

But tempers escalate. They shout over me, over Eddie. At some point, Nana comes waddling in, bleary-eyed and confused about all the ruckus. Asher and Richard sling curses at one another. It's so loud my ears start to ring. We're a kettle on the stove, boiling over— screeching. Richard raises his fist out of anger.

And that's when I see it.

Chet. Yelling at me. The rage in his eyes.

I know Richard is aiming for Asher and not me, but I don't care. Something triggers inside me. A gut reaction. I refuse to let anyone get hurt. This madness has to stop, and this time, I'm going to be brave enough to face it head on.

"Stop it!" I scream at the top of my lungs, throwing myself in the way.

Thankfully, Richard's fist never connects. He comes back to his senses just in time, throwing his momentum to the side instead of forward. He ends up slipping and takes me along with him, too little room or time for me to maneuver out of the way. We both end up on the floor of the living room, Richard's arms wrapped around me. He's shaking, breathing hard.

"Fuck," he rasps. His face drains of color, horror weighing down his features. "Are you—Winona, I didn't—"

"What the fuck is wrong with you?" Eddie roars, quickly helping me to my feet.

I'm crying. At least, I think I'm crying. My cheeks are certainly wet and my nose is all plugged up. I swear it's not because I'm scared of Richard. I know he didn't mean to frighten me. I stepped into the middle of their fight.

Richard scrambles to his feet, nothing but regret written all over his face. "Winona, I didn't mean—Shit."

"I'm fine," I say, wiping my eyes dry. "I just need a moment."

I barrel up the stairs to my guest room.

CHAPTER 19

RICHARD

My mother always used to say I had my father's temper. And in moments like these, I realize how right she was. I've done such a good job of keeping myself in check, of staying in control. I refuse to end up like him, and I hate the thought of resembling my father in any way, shape, or form.

I have utterly failed.

I knock on Winona's door softly, three raps of my knuckles against the solid wood. If I strain, I can just make out the sound of her soft sniffles.

"Winona?" I call out, hating how unsure I sound in my own ear. I'm better than this. More confident, surer. But where Winona's concerned, it's like I'm walking on eggshells. Everything about her has me on edge, my sanity a thin wire drawn taut and on the verge of snapping.

"Come in," she says weakly.

I enter her room and find her seated on the edge of the bed in the middle of wiping her own tears. My chest tightens. I hate myself for upsetting her like this. "Are you alright?" I ask. It's a stupid question, because clearly, she isn't.

"I'm fine," she lies. "Just needed a second to calm down."

I gesture toward the empty space beside her. "May I?"

She nods, patting the blankets to invite me over. The whole mattress dips under my weight, the springs creaking angrily in protest as I settle down next to her. Winona does that little thing with her knees, knocking them gently against my own. It's her way of silently greeting me, telling me it's okay to get close without having to say it aloud.

My throat is unbearably tight as I cast my eyes to the floor. "About what happened down there..."

"It's alright, Richard."

"No, it's not. I'm sorry, Winona."

"Nothing happened."

"It *could* have."

"But it didn't." She peers up at me, holds my gaze. "You didn't hurt me, Richard. And I know that wasn't your intention."

She's trying to let me off the hook, but I won't let her. "I still shouldn't have reacted the way I did. I should have been better than that."

Winona reaches out and takes my hand, threading her fingers between mine. She's so damn small, my hand engulfing hers completely. "I know this is stressful," she says, "but if we put our heads together, there's nothing we can't achieve."

She's so sweet and naive, but it's not really a bad thing. Far from it, in fact. This is a cold, harsh world. I've seen horrors beyond most people's comprehension. I've seen cruelty and violence firsthand. It's easy to get bogged down in the darkness, in the never-ending bitterness. It's easy to get lost in it. But with Winona, she's a beacon of hope. A ray of sunshine. All I want is to protect her innocence and her optimism. I want to make her *smile*.

Because at the end of the day, that's all I want for anyone. I joined the Marines to protect my home, my family, my friends. I carry these burdens on my shoulders so they can be at peace. I fight, and will always fight, hoping they never have to.

Winona leans in slightly, her eyes glued to my lips. Her soft breaths tickle my cheek, the warmth of her palm spread across my own. I really want to kiss her, especially since our shared moment by the lake was so rudely interrupted, but...

"Richard," she breathes my name.

I almost give in. *Fuck.* I want nothing more than to kiss her. Have my way with her. "That's not a good idea, Winona."

She frowns slightly. "Why not?"

"Because if I kiss you, I'll want more. And if I get to have more..."

"What?" Winona asks with a curious tilt of her head. "*What,* Richard?"

"If we do this, I don't think I'll ever be able to let you go."

"Then don't let me go," she replies like it's the simplest thing in the world.

"You won't want me, Winona."

"Isn't that my decision to make?"

"I'm nearly twice your age."

"Do you think I care?"

"You should."

She lifts her hands to cup my face, her lips parted just so. "Richard." I love the way she says my name. Maybe a little too much. All I want is to hear her say it again and again. Whisper it, scream it, whimper it while I bring her to the edge over and over.

"I want you," she murmurs against my lips. "I want you, and them, and *us.* Don't you want me, too?"

"You know I do."

"Then show me," Winona pleads.

My resolve melts away in an instant. I can't take it anymore. Fighting my feelings for her is a losing battle—and I really do hate to lose.

I devour her lips like a man starved, throwing my arms around her to pull her flush against me. Is this what madness feels like? Dizzying and all-consuming and so powerful I fear it might knock my soul out of my body. We're ravenous. My fingers tangle in her hair, while she drags her nails down my back over my shirt. I forget how to breathe, how to think. My heart beats so fast I'm worried it could burst at any moment.

I live for every little sound she makes. Winona whimpers when my hand slips beneath her shirt. She moans when I press her against the sheets, pinning her with the weight of my body. I use my knees to nudge hers apart, growling when she hooks her legs around me to give me better access. The world could be on fire and I wouldn't know it, our bodies so bright and hot and burning we could rival the intense summer sun.

Winona claws at my shirt. "Off," she gasps. "Take it off."

I can't help but chuckle. "Patience, Winona."

"I've been more than patient. Please, just—"

I tear off our clothes in a hurry. I'm officially out of mind, so desperate to have her the throb of my cock brings me actual pain. I swiftly part her legs and align myself, plunging in so deeply Winona has to bite my shoulder to keep from screaming.

"*Richard!*"

My name pours off her tongue, a golden elixir I greedily drink up with a deep kiss. I find instant relief as her pussy clenches around my aching shaft, her walls so hot and slick with desire I slide in with no trouble at all. She takes me in stride, our bodies moving with such power and passion the bed moans along with our movements, headboard banging against the adjacent wall. Any attempt at being discreet—and there was frankly none to start with—has officially gone straight out the window.

She's everything I ever could have wanted and more. There's no understanding how right she feels beneath me, how the world—once askew—has now shifted and fallen into place.

"That's it. Just like that. Fuck, you're going to make me come."

"Please," she whines. "Please, Richard, I'm—"

"Are you close? I can feel you getting close."

She gasps, writhes. I read her body and adjust to her cues. I know exactly what Winona needs, and I have every intention of giving it to her.

Just not yet.

Right when she's on the precipice of release, I pull out and roll her onto her belly. I press hard kisses against the crook of her neck, against her shoulder, marking her with my teeth. I can see the love bites my friends have already left on her delicate skin, and it fills me with a rising sense of pride. These marks are proof of how loved Winona is. It's our way of claiming her, a sign that every inch of her body has been attended to.

I drag my hand lovingly down the expanse of her back, taking in every dip and curve. I'm particularly fond of the small birthmark just above her right ass cheek. Discovering it there is better than striking gold. Dipping down, I press a kiss to it, nibbling at her skin. My heart swells when I earn myself a little giggle, breathless and sweet from Winona's lips.

I slide back into her, my pace just as fast and demanding as it was before. She presses her face against the pillow, clutching it to her with tense hands, muffling her sounds of pleasure against the bedspread. And just when I think she's getting close to release—

I pull out again with a huff, clapping her on the ass.

Winona gasps, her toes curling and her back arching. "*Richard,* why—"

"Good things come to those who wait." And then, right up against her ear, "You don't come unless I *say* you can come, understand?"

"Y-yes..."

"Yes what?"

She moans. "Yes, sir!"

I hum contently. "Good girl."

I continue to tease her, bringing her to the edge only to stop short. She kicks and she whines, bucking her hips in obvious frustration and desperation. I almost feel a little bad, but I know she can take it. It will be well worth the wait when I finally give her permission.

"Alright, it's time," I growl against her ear. "Let me feel you come on my cock."

The rest of the world suddenly falls away. Nothing is more important than this moment. She shatters around me, moaning sharply into her pillow as her body twitches with immeasurable pleasure. Everything about Winona is a work of art. From the way her hair falls over her shoulders, to the light pinkness of her cheeks, to the way sweat glistens over her body.

I find release not long after she does, fire flooding through my veins as ecstasy whites my mind while I empty every drop of myself deep inside her body. I didn't realize how much tension I'd been carrying in my muscles until now. Every fiber of my being is suddenly relaxed, melting from the warmth of our bodies and combined bliss.

Everything after that comes easy. Holding her, breathing her in, kissing her until I'm convinced it's the only thing I know how to do. Winona walking into my life—into *our* lives—is frankly nothing short of a miracle. I'm more than aware of how delicate everything is right now. Between the situation we find ourselves in and this unspoken bond we share, there are a million and one things that can go wrong.

But I know she isn't fragile. Far from it. She can handle everything, come what may. Winona is smart and brave and impossibly kind, enduring our roughest moments without hesitation. The guys and I... We're made of hard edges, trained for years to do nothing more than take orders and kill if necessary.

Winona couldn't be more different. She's all things soft and welcoming and lovely. Maybe that's why we've all taken to her so quickly. She balances us out, smooths us over—provides us with an endless stream of adoration we can't help but cherish. There's so much bad in the world, so many evil people and things... But getting to hold her in my arms makes it all worth it.

"Richard?" she whispers.

"Yes?"

"I know things between you and Asher are rough, but I really hope you can be patient with him." She speaks slowly, but clearly.

"I'm sure we'll find a solution but going after one another isn't help-ing. Please try to see where he's coming from."

I take a deep breath, her wise words bringing me a sense of calm. "Alright," I murmur against the crook of her neck. "I'll talk to him."

"Thank you—"

"Wilder!" Eddie shouts from somewhere downstairs. The alarm in his tone makes me sit up, my heart leaping into my throat. "Wilder, get down here! Asher's gone, and so is the laptop!"

CHAPTER 20

WINONA

"**W**hat do you mean he's *gone*?" I ask, hastily pulling on my shirt and smoothing my hair as Richard and I rapidly descend the stairs.

Eddie huffs. "I don't think I can make myself any clearer, sweetheart."

"He said he wanted to take a walk," Tank says, his answer significantly more helpful. "I thought maybe he wanted to blow off steam, you know? I didn't think he'd just bail on us."

"And the laptop?" Richard asks, his words clipped and dripping with anger.

"He must have swiped it while none of us were looking," Eddie mutters bitterly.

Time comes to a standstill. I swear I can feel my heart tearing in two. Why would Asher do this? Doesn't he understand how bad this looks? Could it be...

Could it be because he doesn't care?

Tank hurriedly fishes his phone out of his pocket and dials a number. "He's not answering."

"We have to go after him," I say. "There's no telling what the colonel will do once he gets his hands on Asher. And there's no guaranteeing William's safety, either."

Richard throws me a glance. "Stay here. The three of us are going to try and track him down before he does something stupid."

I step forward, running on pure adrenaline. "I want to help."

"No, Winona. We brought you here in the first place to keep you safe. I mean no offense, but you'd only get in the way."

I deflate a little, shoulders slumping. Richard's right. I don't know the first thing about tracking a person down or how to negotiate with a man on the edge—because that's what Asher is, a man on the edge who's desperate for answers. It's such a cruel shame the one with the answers is also the same person hoping he'll jump.

"We'll be back soon," Eddie says, pressing a quick kiss to my cheek.

"Bring him back," I whisper, pleading with my eyes. "Promise me."

Richard nods, quickly kissing my temple. "You have my word."

Tank rubs the small of my back, dipping in for a full kiss on the lips. "Don't worry, sugar. We'll be back before you know it. In the meantime, Nana will look out for you, alright?"

The three of them file out through the front door, leaving me in stunned silence in the hall. I lean against the wall beside me with a heavy sigh. No matter what I do, I can't wrap my mind around it. What was Asher thinking? Did he really think he could do this alone?

Or maybe... Is there a chance he's been working with the colonel this whole time?

Doubt creeps into my mind, ugly and cold and cloying. It doesn't make any sense. I *know* Asher is a good man, but therein lies the problem. He's a good friend, a good Marine, a good grandson. But once the chips fall and the cards are on the table, where does his allegiance truly lie? Blood is thicker than water, as they say. Is there a chance Asher decided to betray Tank, Eddie, and Richard? Why else would he leave so suddenly, and with the only incriminating evidence against his grandfather? I've spent this whole time thinking it was impossible. Asher wouldn't do that. Deep within my soul, I've never been surer of it.

And yet...

Would an innocent man run?

A scared one might.

Standing on the porch, I watch as they climb into a farm truck and quickly disappear from sight. Anxiety fills my stomach, churning uncomfortably. This is turning out to be one hell of a summer.

"Goodness," Nana cries as she walks up to me. "What was all that hullabaloo about? I heard everything, and I was out feeding the horses! Where did those boys go?"

"They're, uh..." I search my mind. I'm not too sure how much to tell her. The last thing I want is for Nana to worry, too. "They just had to step out for a bit."

"And they left you all by your lonesome?"

"It had something to do with business," I say with a weak shrug.

Nana pats my wrist. "Why don't you spend some time with me out on the farm? You look like you've got sturdy bones. Feel like helping me with a little heavy lifting?"

I manage a kind smile. In many ways, she and Tank are a lot alike. Always on the go and impossible to say no to. "I'd love to help."

I'm actually grateful Nana asked me to accompany her around the farm. The work is a welcome distraction from all the chaos we've been going through. Nana introduces me to each and every one of her horses, the couple of cows she keeps, as well as all her goats, rabbits, ducks, and chickens.

"You take care of all of them by yourself?" I ask, tossing a handful of feed toward the fowl. They peck away at the ground hungrily, efficiently picking up every morsel.

"Oh, yes," she says, beaming with pride. "It takes me most of the day now, but honest work keeps me young. My husband used to help me with the horses, but Mike's long since passed."

"I'm sorry."

"No, no," Nana says with a gentle smile and a dismissive wave of the hand. "No need to be sorry. That's just life. Besides, I'm sure my sugar's waiting for me beyond those pearly gates. We'll party it up when my time comes."

I grin as she talks. Hearing her refer to her husband as *sugar* reminds me an awful lot of Tank. I wouldn't be surprised if he picked up the endearment from being around her all the time.

"So, how long have you been a thing?" Nana asks. "You and my Joseph?"

"Oh, well... it's a little complicated."

"Because you're in love with the other three, too?"

I pause, casting her with a surprised look. "That's, uh... We're kind of..."

Nana simply throws her head back and laughs. "That's alright, dear. No need to explain. I was just teasing you. I've never been the type to stick my nose where it doesn't belong. But..." She bumps her hip against mine with a cheeky grin. "You're one lucky girl. My eyesight may be going, but I can see as clear as day how they're all smitten with you."

I laugh off my embarrassment and ignore the warmth flooding my cheeks. "You think so?"

"Oh, I *know* so."

"You don't think it's... strange?"

"Sugar, my opinion ain't worth a salt lick. As long as you and those handsome boys are happy, then who cares? Just promise me you'll take good care of them all, especially my Joseph. They're frankly lucky to have such a lovely belle like you."

I nod, adamant and full of resolve. "I'll do my best."

"Did they say what time they'd be home for dinner?"

"I don't think they did."

"Well, that's alright. Let's head back inside and I can get started. I'm thinking a nice big roast with honey-glazed veggies."

My mouth waters at the sound. "That sounds wonderful. Can I help in any way?"

"Are you much of a baker?"

"I love to bake, actually."

Nana beams. "Then I'm putting you in charge of dessert. Joseph used to go wild for my apple tartlets. They're perfect for the summertime. I'll get you a recipe and—"

I pause, sniffing the air. "Wait a moment."

"What is it, dear?"

Taking a deep breath, I note the smell of burning wood and something bitter, something I can't quite place.

"Do you get a lot of campers out in this area?" I ask Nana.

"No. The property extends well past the actual fencing. People aren't supposed to be anywhere near here."

I sniff the air again. Something's wrong, but I'm not quite sure what. I turn to face the main house at the very top of the hill, and I see it. The first few clouds of black smoke and the red and orange flicker of flames.

"Something's burning!" I gasp.

Nana's mouth drops open. "Goodness!"

"Stay here," I tell her. "If it's a small fire, I'll try to put it out."

"Be careful, dear!"

I rush forward, my legs working double time to carry me up the steep hill. As I approach the house, I'm deeply alarmed to find the fire is twice as big as I first imagined. It spreads up the side of the building, catching easily in the grueling summer heat. Something tells me this fire isn't natural. No stray sparks, no reflected sunlight through glass. Once I get closer, I'm finally able to place the strange smell I picked up earlier.

Gasoline.

I look around frantically, searching for any signs, any clues. When I spot four black -clad figures near the house, I hit the deck as fast as I can to remain out of sight. I army crawl to hide behind the trunk of a large tree, curling in to make myself as small as possible.

"Where are they?" a man asks, gruff and forceful.

"No signs of any of them," someone responds.

"The woman?"

"No sign of her, either."

"The fire will smoke them out," a third says, a woman this time.

"They'll be back," the first answers. "And we'll be waiting."

My heart beats so furiously I swear it's going to knock itself loose from within my ribcage.

I hold my breath, clenching my clammy palms to my chest. If I had to venture a guess, I'd say these people are following the orders of the colonel. It's the only logical answer. Maybe Colonel Grey got tired of waiting and decided to strike before the guys could come to a decision. I'm not sure whether to be relieved or afraid they left to chase after Asher. I'd hate to think what would happen to them if they were here.

Keeping as quiet and still as possible, I attempt to peak out from behind the tree. It's hard to get a good look at them. They're all clad from head-to-toe in black, their faces obscured by reflective sunglasses. I see no identifying markers like piercings or tattoos. All I can register is there are four of them and they're all heavily armed. Pistols and machine guns.

Whoever they are, they mean business.

I'm a sitting duck here, and there's a good chance the colonel's team will search the area. The only thing I can think to do is get back to Nana, escape together, and try to find a way to warn the guys. But the chances of getting to a vehicle with these mercenaries in the way... I don't like my odds.

Behind me, I hear the horses whinny as the smoke starts to grow thick and black. An idea suddenly occurs to me. It's crazy and it's ill-planned, but desperate times call for desperate measures.

As quiet as a mouse, I slip away and dash back down the hill to the barn.

"What's going on?" Nana asks, brows knitted together in concern.

"We need to leave," I say hurriedly. "*Now.*"

CHAPTER 21

EDDIE

No matter how many times I try calling, Asher won't pick up his phone.

There's a good chance he's turned it off.

Fuck.

"This isn't good," Tank mumbles.

"Yeah, no shit," I shoot back.

"He's probably already hit the highway," Richard says. "We won't be able to catch up with him in time."

"It's not like it's a straight shot from here to Seattle. He has to stop at some point for gas, doesn't he?"

There are too many variables at play here, not to mention the clock is ticking down. I won't pretend to be ignorant of Asher's motivations. I've known the man for many years, and that's why I know it couldn't have been an easy decision for him to leave us like this. Asher is a good man, an honorable man.

But even good and honorable men can break.

And I'm spiraling along with him.

I'd be lying if I said I'm alright, because honestly? I swear to God my head is two seconds away from exploding. Those emails were the only thing keeping the colonel from making a move. Now that we no longer have any leverage against him, there's nothing standing in his way from taking us out from afar. We may be in a moving vehicle, but a trained sniper could easily take us out while we're on the freeway. I should know. I've done it before.

It's only a matter of when and where the colonel finally decides to dispose of us.

"We need to get back to Winona," I say, my voice almost drowned out by the angry roar of the truck and the wind whipping over the hood. "Things are about to get ugly. We need to go into hiding."

"She's secure at the farm," Tank insists. "Nobody knows she's there."

"Asher does."

Richard shoots me a cold glare. "You think he'd tell his grandfather about her?"

"I don't know. Before, I would have trusted him with her life. With *all* our lives. Now..."

"We need to lie low for a while," Tank adds. "Go into hiding."

"What?" Richard snaps. "You want to hide like fucking cowards?"

"What other option is there?"

"What about William?"

"There's nothing we can do now. We're in over our heads."

"He may be retired, but our policy still stands—no man left behind."

And we're bickering again, unable to come up with a feasible answer. Tank raises his voice, Richard raises his voice louder, and I...

I'm drowning on dry land. The more we struggle, the more I realize there's no escape. We're dead men walking, and it's only a matter of time before the colonel walks us right into our graves. This is a no-win scenario. Sometimes I wonder if I really died the day we failed our mission and this is just some cyclical torture in Hell. Because every breath I take now is a struggle, anxiety and frustration seeping out of every pore. I don't know how much more of this night-mare I can take.

Behind the wheel, Richard's shoulders slump. We've been on the road for hours, trying and failing to track Asher down. There's no point in denying it—we've lost.

"Fuck," he mumbles, making a sharp U-turn to head back to the farm. "Eddie, call Winona. Let her know we're on the way back. I'm sure she's worried."

I pull out my phone and dial her number, but the call rings at least six or seven times before it goes to voicemail. I try again and then again, but she doesn't answer.

"Something's wrong," I say dryly. I can't ignore the sinking feeling in my stomach. Things have already gone from bad to worse to terrible. If something's happened to Winona, I swear I'll burn the whole world to the ground.

Without another word, Richard slams on the gas pedal.

～

Fire.

I see and smell the smoke well before I see the flames, but it none-theless makes me want to puke. That rat bastard Colonel Grey thought he could attack us while our backs were turned? How low can that motherfucker go? Despite the chaos inside my skull, despite the rage boiling inside me, there's only one thought on my mind.

Winona.

As we pull up, we spot a black SUV parked beyond the front gate of the farm. Tank is already lifting out of his seat, his knuckles stark white as he rips off his seatbelt, practically ready to throw himself out of the vehicle. I count four enemies, all heavily armed. The fire rages behind them, consuming what little remains of the smoldering farm-house. And we were hoping to lay low for a while. It seems they've brought the fight right to our front yard.

"Hang on tight!" Richard roars as he stomps on the gas, the engine screaming loudly as we careen forward at the group of mercs.

Three of them manage to jump out of the way in time, but one poor son of a bitch isn't nearly as lucky. There's no describing the sound his body makes when it hits the front of the truck, tumbles up over the windshield, and goes flying out of view. There's no question about it—he's dead.

Now we've evened the playing field.

Outside, there's shouting. The mercs scream commands at one another, shouting to get to cover as they duck behind trees. They're quick to fire, drawing their weapons and unloading a storm of bullets.

Tank, Richard, and I knew it was coming. We all hit the deck, staying as low as possible as we scramble out of the truck together. None of us have weapons; they're at the farmhouse, but we are ready for the fight .

With my belly flat against the earth, I throw a cautious glance over my shoulder as we brave the oncoming gunfire. I spot the log chopping area next to the woodshed, a sharp ax embedded into an old stump. The metal looks dull, the handle worn down from years of use —but a weapon is a weapon, and in my hands, anything can be made deadly.

My training comes back to me all at once. I breathe deeply, banishing my panic and fear. There will be plenty of time to freak out later, the devils of my mind ready to tear me to shreds. Until then, I only have three goals: protect my friends, get out of this alive, and find Winona.

Suddenly, silence.

The mercs have run out of ammunition. I can hear frustrated grunts and the rapid clicks of their loosened magazines. I have maybe thirty seconds, tops. So I run. Pushing myself off the ground, I dash toward the ax, grab it by its handle, and yank it out of the stump. I see them from across the way, my eyes trained on the three mercs like a homing beacon. Now only one question remains: can I take them out before they can riddle me full of holes? There's no time to think about it, only to *do*.

Something inside my brain finally breaks. I've been teetering on the edge, my thoughts swarming with shadows. Now there's nothing to hold it back. I'm overcome with a violent, uncontrollable rage. The only way to ensure these people won't hurt me is if I hurt them first.

I lunge at the nearest attacker, swinging the ax over my head. It lands with a wet thud, nailing him right in the shoulder. He screams, but I don't hear him. I can't hear anything. I'm too consumed with my need to take him down to care about his cries for mercy. I'm too afraid of what he might do to Richard or Tank. I'm petrified at the thought of what he's already done to Winona and Tank's poor nana.

Are they somewhere inside the house, trapped by the blaze? Or did they manage to find a way out? I need to get to them, no matter the cost.

Someone grabs me from behind, wrapping their arm around my throat to lock me in a chokehold. The man I managed to hit with the ax stumbles back, clutching his injury with a squeaky wail. A third attacker nails me right in the gut, the pain knocking the air from my lungs. Out of the corner of my eye, I see the silver glint of a combat knife. He goes for my jugular—

But not before Richard swoops in and drives his knee right into the attacker's nose. I'd find the crunch of his bones satisfying were I not so preoccupied with survival. Richard wrestles the knife-wielder to the ground while I drive my head back, effectively headbutting my captor as hard as I can. His hold around my throat loosens, and it's frankly all I need to turn things around.

My knuckles meet his jaw. His nails scrape at my cheek. He goes for his gun, but I kick it out of reach. The entire time, I'm vaguely aware of how Richard and Tank are doing. Richard's holding his own fine, but Tank is struggling. He may have his size, but his bad arm puts him at a disadvantage. He's pinned, struggling, gasping for air. I know I have to end this quickly, so I knock my assailant out with all the brute force I can muster. With a swift punch, he's out like a light.

"Tank!" I shout, rapidly stumbling onto my feet before throwing myself at his attacker.

It's a woman who's got him pinned, a pair of brass knuckles bruising Tank up like no one's business. I was always raised to believe you should never hit a woman, but those rules don't apply when it comes to life and death. I yank her back by the hair, seething through gritted teeth.

"Where's the woman?" I hiss against her ear. "What did you do to Winona?"

"Let go of me, you son of a bitch!" she shrieks, like *I'm* the one in the wrong for going on the defensive.

"Enough!" someone's sharp command slices through the air.

Tank and I turn to see Richard on his knees, both his hands up in the air in surrender. Behind him, one of the mercenaries clad in black has a pistol pointed at the base of Richard's skull, a twitchy finger wrapped around the trigger.

"Release her," the man snaps at me.

I do so. Not because I'm feeling merciful, but because I really don't want to see Richard meet his maker. This brings back too many bad memories. All I can remember is the explosion, the confusion, the horror when we realized it was too late to turn back. We lost three good men that day—and I refuse to see yet another taken from me.

"You put up a good fight, I'll give you that much," the man says. He doesn't speak with an ounce of emotion. Everything about him is cold and distant, though I don't think he's trying to be particularly cruel. We're just strangers to him, nothing more than a job. But his indifference makes everything worse. There's no point in pleading, in begging for our lives because he doesn't care. Impassable.

"What do you want with us?" Tank asks, spitting out the blood coating his teeth.

"On your feet. Colonel Grey would like to speak with you."

CHAPTER 22

WINONA

I went to horse riding camp one summer many, *many* years ago, but I surprise myself with how easily all my lessons come rushing back to me. After helping Nana onto the back of one of her horses, I made sure to free the rest from the barn just in case the fire spread. I'd hate to see any of these innocent creatures get hurt. Once I'm convinced we're a safe distance away, I tell Nana to continue on her own.

"Do you think you can make it to one of your neighbors?" I ask her.

"I should be able to. The Andersons live a couple of miles this way."

I nod hurriedly. "When you get there, be sure to call 9-1-1 as soon as you can."

"What about you?"

"I have to warn the guys before they come back," I say. I've been trying to call them on my cell, but we're so isolated I haven't been able to get a signal.

"What if those awful people catch you?" Nana asks, clearly horrified.

"I'll keep out of sight, I promise. I just need to get close enough to the house where I can get enough bars."

"Be careful," she warns before snapping the leather reins in her hands.

I pat my own horse on the side of her neck. "Come on, girl. Let's get a move on."

She rides well, the mare's strong legs carrying us forward. She makes it back up the steep hill no problem, no doubt happy to stretch her legs. From where we are, I can see the SUV is still there... Along with a second vehicle. The guys.

I hastily dismount and send the horse on her way, hoping she's smart enough to run in the opposite direction of the fire. I keep low to the ground, sticking to the tree line. As I approach, I can hear the angry sounds of an all-out fight.

"Where's the woman?" Eddie hisses. "What did you do to Winona?"

My heart leaps into my throat. Instinct tells me to cry out, to tell them I'm fine and I'm here. But that'd give away my position. It's too dangerous to reveal myself now. All I can do is watch as one of the mercenaries holds a gun to the back of Richard's head, not a hint of remorse to be found.

Every inch of my body suddenly goes cold. Am I about to watch him be murdered? Fear shreds through my lungs, incapacitating me from head to toe. I can't bear to watch, yet I can't bring myself to look away. They're talking, Tank and this mercenary. I'm too far away to hear, but before I know it, Tank, Eddie, and Richard are quickly being escorted into the back of the waiting SUV.

Their wrists are bound, their ankles tied up, their mouths gagged with dirty cloth. It all happens so quickly, clearly a practiced, perfunctory thing for these people. Within thirty seconds, they gather their fallen comrade and climb into their vehicle, shifting into gear so abruptly the gravel kicks out from beneath the tires.

I move as fast as I'm able, digging my fingers into the dirt and grass as I scramble to my feet. The truck the guys were driving is still running, the keys in the ignition. I have no plan, no strategy. All I know is I have to tail them for as long as possible. They've done everything they can to protect me—and now I want to return the favor.

I climb into the front seat of the car, put on my seatbelt, and pull a very sloppy three-point turn before barreling down the road. I'm a good distance away, but I can see the SUV up ahead. Losing them on the highway isn't an option. Ensuring I keep enough space between us without losing track of them is now my top priority. If they figure out I'm following them, it's all over.

So I make sure to leave a few cars between us, always sticking to just above the speed limit so as to not draw any attention to myself. The SUV I'm tailing doesn't drive erratically, doesn't weave in and out of lanes—most likely for the exact same reason. If the highway patrol were to pull them over only to find their hostages in the back of the vehicle, I'm sure it wouldn't go well for the driver, hence playing it safe.

I'm on the edge of my seat the whole time, my grip on the steering wheel so tight my knuckles start to ache and throb from the pressure. I don't think my heart has ever been under this much stress for such a long time. It occurs to me that I don't have a next step. What happens when they finally stop? I have no weapons on me, I don't know how to fight. There's no doubt in my mind that the colonel is the one behind this, but I can't call the cops for help because then there'd be no stopping him from hurting the guys or my brother.

There has to be some way to stop him, and if not, surely there's something I can do to buy us a little time. My men are capable, strong, and brave. They're not just going to lie down and take this injustice. Knowing them, they're already cooking up an escape plan. And if I can help even the odds, even just a bit, then I'll consider it a job well done.

～

I've been on the highway for roughly twelve hours now, driving under the cover of nightfall, having only stopped for gas once at the same time the SUV did. I'm about to run on empty, and I'm sure the vehicle in front of me is too.

So when they finally pull into what looks like a secluded, decommissioned landing strip, I breathe a sigh of relief. For a moment, I think the hard part is over. When I park the car and kill the lights several yards away, slumping down low to keep out of sight, I realize the hard part is only just beginning.

Now what am I supposed to do?

Tank, Eddie, and Richard's captors are quick to escort them into a nearby hangar. Everything about this place screams decay and isolation, forgotten to the annals of time. Something tells me nobody's going to be stumbling through the area by accident. I've read and edited enough spy and horror novels to know a place like this is the perfect location to make someone disappear.

Once I'm sure the coast is clear, I get out of the truck and keep low. I shift my eyes left to right, searching for any surveillance cameras, guards, dogs, anything that might blow my cover. But I see nothing. There's nothing standing in my way except for the armed assailants holding the guys hostage. It's pretty clear to me this is a discrete operation with few individuals involved. The colonel probably doesn't want to clean up any more loose ends.

When I finally make it to the hangar, I don't go in through the main entrance for obvious reasons. I slink through the shadows like a creature of the night and manage to find a back door to the hangar. There's a hefty lock keeping it shut, rust covering the entirety of its surface.

It'd be easy to give up, to admit defeat, but I've come too far to give up now. Looking around, I try to find something I can use to bash the lock. I'm going to have to be quick. Time is of the essence, and the more time I waste, the closer to death the guys will be.

Before I make more noise than can be ignored, I try the knob. I am shocked to find it unlocked, and I slowly open the door so there's no noise. Thankfully, nobody comes. I open the door wide enough to slip inside the hangar.

The smell inside is unpleasant, to say the least. Dusty and moldy, the air is thick with stale moisture. It's crowded, stuffed full with old shelves and abandoned supplies. I wonder if this hangar was temporarily transformed into some sort of storage warehouse. It's dark, too. I don't think the electricity works in this place, which is actually helpful. As long as I keep out of sight, I'm safe.

Somewhere off in the distance, I hear the murmur of voices.

I venture forward, every step careful and quiet. Staying behind a tall shelf, I peek through a few of the rotten boxes and find five men strapped to chairs, illuminated only by the faint light of the moon and the harsh glow of a powerful flashlight. It takes every ounce of my strength not to cry or scream.

Asher.

Tank.

Eddie.

Richard.

William.

Confusion swirls inside my skull, leaving me lightheaded. My fight or flight response is going off like crazy, but my feet are glued in place. What's Asher doing here? I thought he left... Unless he didn't? And how long has my brother been here? He looks worse for wear, roughed up and exhausted. I have to bite my tongue, the pain keeping me grounded in reality. If those assholes hurt my brother, there's going to be hell to pay.

Standing before him is a man I've only seen on FaceTime. He's not dressed in a uniform, but he doesn't have to be for me to know he's a Marine. It's in the ram-rod straight posture of his back. It's in the severity of his scowl.

Colonel George Grey.

What the hell is he doing in Alabama? Wasn't he in Seattle? My questions go unanswered when I hear Asher's voice.

"Let them go!" Asher pleads. "Gramps, please... Do whatever you want to me, but let my friends go."

"They'll talk," the colonel says simply.

"No, they won't. I'll make them promise."

"Don't be stupid, boy. You think I can be convinced by something as flimsy as a promise?"

"They're men of their word," Asher continues. "Men of honor. They're Marines, for Christ' sake! If you agree to let them go, I guarantee they won't say anything."

"I *do* like guarantees," the colonel says, reaching behind him to brandish a pistol. He aims it directly at Eddie's forehead and pulls back the hammer. "And there's no better guarantee than putting you all six feet under."

Eddie doesn't even flinch. "Fuck you. Fucking do it, you coward!"

I hold my breath. What the hell is he doing? Has he lost his mind?

The colonel only smiles, cold and cruel. He lowers his weapon with a small shrug. "I'd rather not get my hands dirty."

Tank spits. "Pussy."

"I'd watch what you say to me, Quill."

Tank laughs, loud and bitter. "Or what? You'll burn down my childhood home? Oh, wait... You already did that, huh?"

"I regret that my team had to go so far. It was never my intention to drag your poor grandmother into this."

At the mere mention of Nana, Tank stills. His face is suddenly ghostly white. The colonel notices this and smiles even wider.

"Tell me, Quill, how are those sisters of yours doing?"

"Don't you fucking dare—"

"I just want to know one thing," the colonel interrupts, addressing all his captives. He snaps his fingers and one of his lackeys, the man who had Richard at gunpoint earlier, steps forward with a laptop.

The laptop.

"Have you made any copies I should be aware of?" Colonel Grey asks. "Did Denise send my private correspondence to anyone else? Tell me the truth, and I won't have my people pay your sisters a visit."

I suck in a careful breath and slowly reach into my pocket for my phone. I might be able to use this. The entire time, I've been waiting for an opportunity to strike, but now I realize I need to *make* an opportunity. I quickly punch in Richard's number—if he still has it on him, great; if they took it off him, even better.

A few short seconds later, his phone goes off.

The colonel casts an annoyed glare over his shoulder at one of his other lackeys. She fishes through her pockets and pulls out Richard's cell.

"Who's calling?" Richard asks.

"Someone called Winona," the woman answers.

CHAPTER 23

ASHER

"Answer it," my grandfather says, "and put it on speaker." I hold my breath, so enraged I think my blood might boil me alive. After our argument at the farmhouse, I decided to take a long drive to cool my head. I couldn't forgive myself for dragging Winona into our fight. I hoped the quiet and fresh air would help. The only reason I took the laptop with me was because the guys went to separate parts of the house, and I didn't want to leave it unattended.

And that's when they nabbed me.

I should have known I was being watched. It all happened too fast for me to react. They forced the minivan off the road, threw a gag in my mouth and a hood over my head before throwing me to the ground and tying me up like a hog. They threw me into the back of a car, mentioning something about sending a second team to grab the rest of the guys later.

The colonel wants this one brought in alive.

Kill the others if you have to.

"Winona Wren," the colonel greets, a hint of amusement in his tone. "I've learned so much about you lately, it feels like I've known you forever."

"Release them," she says flatly. "*All* of them."

"You think you can make demands of me?"

"I know I can."

"And why is that?"

"Because I have a copy of your emails. Several, in fact."

I glance at Eddie, who's tied up in the chair beside me. When did Winona have time to do that? Is she... Oh, God, is she *bluffing*?

"I think you're lying, Ms. Wren."

"Fuck around and find out, asshole. I have copies of the incriminating emails scheduled to send to the *New York Times*, CNN, the *Wall Street Journal*... You name it. It's done automatically, set on a timer that will forward everything unless I manually cancel. So if you try to do anything to the guys or to my brother, I'll let the timer run out and you're fucked."

I study my grandfather's face carefully. It's strange, seeing him in this new light. My whole life, I've loved and adored this man. He was more than a caretaker; he was a mentor and a father-figure. Knowing he was behind all of this, knowing now—without a shadow of a doubt—that he's been the one behind these awful attacks... It makes me sick to my stomach. I guess you can never truly understand a person, and that fact alone makes me unbearably sad.

The colonel's left eye twitches. It's a subtle reaction, barely noticeable. But I was raised by this man, lived under the same roof as him for many years—even joined the Marines to follow his command. The little eye twitch may seem inconsequential, but I know the truth: Winona's gotten under his skin. I think he's on the verge of buying her lie.

"You heard her," I say. "Release us and we can all walk away like nothing ever happened. We'll go our separate ways and forget all about this."

He's quiet for a long time, as rigid and still as a statue carved from stone. It's impossible to tell what's going on inside his head. After a while, though, he turns to his merc and nods. "Find her. I have a feeling she's close. The timing of that call was too perfect."

I gulp hard. Shit, he's probably right.

The colonel's lackeys peel off, drawing their weapons as they begin a sweep of the hangar. I silently pray Winona's already on the move.

"Why did you do it?" I ask. "Why did you betray us? What could have possibly been worth selling us out?"

My grandfather tilts his head to the side and regards me with a bored expression. "Do you know how many years I've given to this country?"

I'm not sure if I'm supposed to answer or not, so I opt for silence. I need to hear the truth straight from his mouth, and I have no plans on interrupting his train of thought.

"Forty-seven years," he says slowly, thoughtfully. "I signed up when I was eighteen and gave them almost five decades of my life. And do you know what they gave me in return?"

I chew on the inside of my cheek, struggling to keep my comments to myself. "What?" I grumble.

"PTSD, several measly promotions, a laughable pension, and all of my closest friends buried with their flags." My grandfather's nostrils flare, his stare suddenly distant and vacant. "I missed so much. The birth of my daughter, your mother. All her birthdays, the day she graduated from college. And then the accident... I was overseas when it happened, fighting in yet another meaningless war because the Corps ordered me to do so. Do you know what it feels like? To be that helpless and a world away, when all you want is to be with family?"

I grit my teeth, struggling not to let his words get to me. My grandfather rarely mentions my mother. After the funeral, I was whisked away into his care. After that, it was like she didn't even exist. He took down all her photos, squirreled them away up in the attic. I couldn't understand it then, and I can only barely understand it now. The colonel was in so much pain he would rather ignore it.

"After all I've given..." he murmurs. "We're saddled with so much. We carry the weight of our crimes, and for what? Veterans are treated like trash, left to fend for themselves. We're given a shiny new medal every now and then, but that's it. Nobody cares about what happens to us, only what we can do for them. So why have any qualms about taking what we want for ourselves?"

"So you did this for money?" Richard hisses. "You greedy son of a—"

"How much?" I ask, my soul withering on the inside.

"Fifty million dollars."

The number is so massive I can't even begin to wrap my head around it. It doesn't even sound like a real number when said aloud. Judging by the appalled looks on my friends' faces, they're reeling along with me.

"Who'd you sell them out to?" William pipes up. His voice is hoarse and scratchy, likely from hours spent yelling.

"They were supposed to capture a high-value target," the colonel says casually. "But the father of the target reached out to me, as I'm sure you're aware thanks to Denise's lack of discretion. He offered me the payout in exchange for the mission details. Who, what, where, when... I didn't have to lift a finger. All that was required on my end was to give him and his team enough of a heads-up."

Eddie lurches in his seat. "You bastard! Our men are dead because of you."

"It's regrettable, truly."

Tank scowls furiously. "But you knew Asher was assigned to the mission. Are you really so cold as to risk his life?"

"I asked that he specifically be left alive. I wasn't counting on all four of you making it out, yet here you are. How very fortunate for all of you."

Anger doesn't even begin to describe the fury burning in my chest. I'm a firestorm, a hurricane thunderclap. Every word out of this man's mouth kills me, only to zap me back to life so I can suffocate in my own rage. I can't believe what I'm hearing. I don't *want* to believe it. But every passing moment, I'm forced to confront the cold, hard truth: the colonel, my own grandfather, my flesh and blood, really is every ounce a conniving, heartless traitor.

"Don't look at me like that," he admonishes. "You can still get out of this alive."

I can't bear to meet his eyes. He doesn't deserve the base-level respect of eye contact. "If you're going to kill us, kill *all* of us. I'd rather die with my platoon than let you get away with this."

"You're being too rash, Asher. Think of it. I have the money now. We can both retire and go our separate ways if you want, but you'll never have to worry about a thing. Isn't that what family does? We take care of each other, no matter what."

"You're not my family," I growl through gritted teeth. "These men here... *They're* my family. I know they'd never betray me—unlike you."

The colonel takes a deep breath, taking a step back to fix his posture. He casts a cold, indifferent glare down his nose at me. Disappointment weighs heavily on his face. "Very well. Don't say I didn't give you a chance. You've made your bed, and now you must lie in it."

"Fuck you and your speeches," I snap. "If you're going to shoot us, hurry up and do it."

"I'll deal with you all soon," the colonel vows. "Just as soon as I find that pretty little sister of yours, Wren. Once I've dealt with her, *then* I'll put a bullet between your eyes."

"You keep your fucking hands off my sister," William spits.

With a huff, my grandfather turns on his heels and leaves, taking the only true source of light with him. The five of us are in the dark, nothing but the sound of our heavy breathing and frantic hearts to fill the cavernous void of the hangar.

"Well," William mutters. "This fucking sucks."

"We need to get out of here," Richard says.

"No fucking shit," Eddie replies with a groan.

"Winona must be close," Tank comments. "The colonel was

right. The timing of that call was too perfect. I bet she was within earshot."

"They didn't get their hands on her at Nana's house, did they?" I ask.

"No, I don't think so."

"Better fucking not," Eddie huffs.

"Wait. Why would my sister be here risking her life for you guys?" William asks.

Silence lulls over us for a moment.

"Can we please deal with one problem at a time?" Tank asks.

"He's right," Richard says. "Our priority is getting out of here and making sure Win's safe. We need to *think*."

"Hey, Eddie?" I call out.

"What?"

"Do you still know how to dislocate your thumbs?"

He makes a disagreeable sound. "Yes, but it hurts."

"Quit bitchin'," Tank says. "You've got to slip out of those cuffs somehow."

"*Fine*," Eddie grumbles, followed by a swift and distressingly loud pop and a groan.

CHAPTER 24

WINONA

O h my God, oh my God, oh my *God*.

Running normally isn't a problem for me. It's usually my go-to form of exercise. When Chet and I used to get into an argument, I'd go for a jog to blow off some steam. The rhythmic pounding of my sneakers against the pavement is calming, the rocking motion of my arms as I swing them back and forth enjoyable. Running is fun...

Just not when I'm being chased by two armed mercenaries with loaded weapons and instructions to capture me. This is a deadly game of cat and mouse, and I'm unfortunately an unwilling participant.

To say I'm at a disadvantage in every way is an understatement. I don't have the stamina to keep going forever. I'm not familiar with the area or the terrain. I have no fighting skills whatsoever, so if they catch me, I'm done for. At least it's a small comfort knowing the colonel took my threat seriously. If he wastes time trying to catch me, then that's time I've afforded the guys so they can hopefully escape.

My lungs burn. The muscles in my thighs are cramping. It feels like I'm stuck in a nightmare, running so hard but going nowhere at all. I can hear them, my pursuers—only a few paces behind me now.

They're going to reach me soon if I don't do something drastic. It's frankly a wonder they haven't shot me yet. Maybe because the colonel wants me brought to him alive? I did say those emails would be sent unless I canceled it, after all.

I weave through the trees, nearly trip and fall as I attempt to reach civilization. I see lights up ahead. A city. Maybe I can lose them there. When the soles of my shoes hit hard concrete, hope sparks within me. I've made it to town, but can I evade the colonel's lackeys here? If I asked for help, would anybody bother to offer it?

I run without thinking, no destination in mind. I take sharp turns around buildings, squeeze through several alleyways, and race through an open-air night market that's surprisingly crowded considering the late hours. I'm officially winded, but I keep going, elbowing my way through the crowd.

Between the sweltering summer heat and the thin, dry air, I can barely breathe. I always come up short, gasping and choking as I urge my body forward. This has to be what dying feels like. No matter how much my mind screams to run, my limbs are nothing more than a tangled mess.

They're behind me. *Right* behind me. I gave it my best shot, but was it good enough? I know I'm not as strong as Asher, Tank, Eddie, or Richard, but I sure as hell like to think I'm just as brave. I *know* I am.

I don't beat myself up when my legs finally give out on the other side of the market, away from the safety of the crowd. I don't curse myself out when the colonel's team gets their hands on me, yanking me upright. I don't allow myself a hint of pity when they drag me away—because I did my best. I'm no superhero, I'm not some be-all end-all it girl. I've been thrown into a situation I wanted no part of and *still* decided to throw myself in headfirst. If that's not something to be proud of, I don't know what is.

~

They take me back to the hangar. My body is numb and sore. It's frankly a miracle I even have the strength to hold myself up. I tell myself it's all worth it, though, because I'm sure the guys—

Are in the exact same spot I left them. *Shit.*

"You were supposed to escape! To run away!" I snap at them, absolutely distraught.

"Sorry, sweetheart," Eddie grumbles, shrugging. "They've got us locked up tight."

"It's going to be alright, sugar," Tank says. "Just keep calm."

"Calm?" I echo incredulously as I'm forced sit across from them in a chair of my own. "How am I supposed to stay calm?"

"Deep breaths, Win," William encourages me. "We've got everything under control."

"Yeah, it looks like it."

"Easy, Winona," Richard says, his tone stern but undeniably warm. "We're really proud of you."

Behind me, a man's low, cold chuckle. The colonel emerges from the shadows like a damn specter, watching our group's interaction with an amused smirk. "So this is the woman I've heard so much about lately. I've had my people keep tabs on you. It's a pleasure to finally meet you in person."

I sneer up at him. "The feeling's not mutual."

The colonel doesn't bother crouching down, but instead towers over me so I have to crane my neck back to get a good look at him. It's an intimidation tactic, one Chet sometimes used when we were in the middle of a disagreement, but I'm not going to let this asshole get the better of me.

"I suppose there's no point in playing nice," the colonel says. "Cancel your scheduled emails."

I sit up a bit straighter. "No."

"Do it."

"Or what?"

"I'll kill each and every one of them while you watch—starting with your brother."

My eyes flick over to William. It's so unbelievably good to see him, but I wish it had been under better circumstances. He looks tired and out of sorts, but all in all in good health.

"Don't give him shit," William tells me. "I'd rather die than see this asshole get away with anything."

The colonel clicks his tongue. "Ah, stupidity runs in the family, I see. Fine then." He pulls out his gun and aims it at Eddie, slowly sweeping his aim over the line to gauge my reaction.

I almost cave. I don't like violence or threats, and seeing this unhinged lunatic point a loaded weapon at the guys nearly sends me over the edge. "Stop it."

"Should I shoot Wilder between the eyes?" he muses. "Or maybe I'll put two bullets square in Luna's chest. Better yet, I can prolong his suffering and shoot Quill's kneecaps before blowing his brains out."

It's a struggle, but I manage not to react to any of the colonel's cruel words. He can't get the better of me. I refuse to give him the satisfaction of getting under my skin.

A wicked look suddenly washes over his face. "Or... maybe I'll have *you* pull the trigger."

I flinch. "What?"

The colonel snatches my wrist and forces his gun into my hand. I try to pull away, but I'm too exhausted and weary. I'm trapped, forced to point the barrel of the gun in Asher's direction.

"Delete those emails, Ms. Wren," he says against my ear. His voice makes my skin crawl. "I know you care for him. I know you care for *all* of them. So do us both a favor and make this easy. Agree to my terms and I won't make you kill them."

I squirm in my seat, my arm shaking as I try to keep the colonel from squeezing my finger on the trigger. "Stop it!"

"All you have to do is say yes."

I choke on my tears. This can't be happening. When will this nightmare end?

"It's okay, angel," Asher says gently, his sweet words cutting through my panic. "We got you."

We got you.

They've told me this over and over again—and each time, it's always true. They've never failed me, and I won't fail them.

With all my might, I throw my hand upward. The momentum catches the colonel off guard. The gun goes off, a bullet screaming up into the air. It leaves a small hole in the roof of the hangar, the loud *bang* echoing loudly off the walls and ceiling.

"Now!" Richard bellows.

The guys lunge from their chairs, revealing that their hands are no longer bound. They must have figured out a way to escape their handcuffs. They're as fast as lightning, moving with practiced precision. Even my brother joins the brawl, his years as a Marine coming back to him without fail.

Eddie and Tank go after the lackeys, while Asher, Richard, and William dive toward the colonel. They're on top of him, three against one. They've got him pinned to the ground, arm twisted behind his back, slapping the very same cuffs that bound them onto the colonel's wrists.

"Release me!" he demands. "Release me at once!"

His cries go unanswered.

William is the first to come to me, wrapping me up in a tight hug. "Are you okay?" my brother asks me.

"Do I *look* okay?" I scream.

"What do you need, Win?"

"I need a damn vacation. A proper one."

William exhales, the corners of his lips curling up into a smile. "Alright, alright. I hear you. No need to shout."

"Sorry. That gunshot was a lot louder than I thought it would be. My eardrums are still ringing."

On the ground, the colonel groans. "Those copies... You were lying, weren't you." He says this like a statement, not a question.

I nod. "My only goal was to stall you."

His nostrils flare. "I've already destroyed Denise's laptop, and I've already had my people erase the private server. All your evidence is destroyed. If you don't unhand me—"

"Your bank account," Asher says quickly.

"What?"

"Even if you destroyed the communication logs, we can still have the money traced back to you," Richard says. "You're as good as fucked, Colonel Grey."

His face turns bright red. "You're all going to regret this. Mark my words, this isn't over. The moment you let your guard down..."

"Shut up," Eddie grumbles. "Fuck, some people love the sound of their own voice."

I breathe a huge sigh of relief as I look at each of them. Nobody's hurt. I'd chalk it up to being a miracle, but I know the truth.

It's because we're one hell of a team.

CHAPTER 25

WINONA

Naturally, Colonel Grey's arrest causes a media firestorm. People want answers, and rightly so. An American service member selling out his own countrymen? It's unforgivable. Between Denise's testimony, the guys' accounts of the mission gone wrong and everything that unfolded afterward, as well as the fifty million dollars sitting in the colonel's offshore accounts, I'm pretty sure this case is a no brainer.

Granted, I don't know much about court-martialing or what to expect from the colonel's upcoming trail, but it's over and done with. Behind me. The trial date isn't for a few months, and until then, I can sleep well at night knowing he's safely behind bars awaiting his sentencing.

Well, I can *almost* sleep well at night.

After helping Nana move in with one of her granddaughters—Tank's eldest sister, Bernice, who only lives a few miles away from the farm—we all drove back to the lake house to lie low and enjoy the summer heat. We briefly considered taking a trip, but because the guys are such important witnesses, the lawyers didn't want us going anywhere we couldn't be reached.

So while I settle in by the lake and soak up the sun as June rolls into July, sandwiched on either side by Eddie and Asher, it's hard to... *do* anything else except lounge there in the sand. Call it paranoia or being a little too careful, but I swear William's been keeping a particularly diligent eye on me ever since we got back.

"Do you think he suspects something?" I ask Asher.

"I can't be sure, sugar, but surely there's no harm in telling him, right?"

I help him apply a bit of sunscreen on the back of his shoulders. The touch is casual, perfectly friendly—but I really want to run my hands all over him. "I don't think that would go over too well," I confess. "William might lose it if he finds out that we... Well."

"That we all enjoy being with you?" Eddie asks, surprisingly delicate with his choice of words.

"That's certainly one way of putting it." I tuck my knees up against my chest. "He's always been very protective of me."

"Just as we are," Asher says sweetly.

I manage a smile. "I don't know. It's just... an awkward conversation to have."

"Then don't have it," Eddie suggests. "We can make our own choices. You don't have to tell your brother everything that goes on in your life. It's not like he's your keeper."

"No, I know. But he's still family and we've always been close. Besides, I don't want to keep you four my dirty little secret. I'm proud to be with you all. I shouldn't have to hide it."

"It's up to you," Asher says. "If you want to talk to him, I support your decision."

"Just be prepared in case he doesn't take the news well," Eddie adds.

Asher tosses him a glare. "*Supportive.*"

"I'm not going to fill her head with false hopes, Grey. She needs to brace herself."

"Eddie's right," I mumble. "It could go either way."

Under the cover of the sand, Asher reaches for my hand and

threads his fingers between mine, giving them a light squeeze. "Just relax, angel. We have time to figure it out together."

"Speaking of, where are the others?" Eddie asks. "Didn't they say they were going to join us?"

"Tank mentioned something about wanting to throw a barbecue for the Fourth of July," I mention. "And something about how 'your fridge isn't big enough to fit that many ribs'."

"*That's* your impression of me?" Tank asks, aghast. He makes his way down the dirt path between the lake house and the water's edge, dressed in swim trunks with a towel slung over his shoulder. Richard and William aren't too far behind, though they seem caught up in their own conversation.

I laugh. "Glad you could finally join us."

"And for the record, your fridge *is* too small. If we're going to celebrate Independence Day, I expect to eat in style."

"How much food are we talking exactly?"

"Only the essentials. Ribs, burgers, hot dogs, couple cases of beer..."

I sigh. "Please tell me you plan on having a few veggies, too."

Tank makes a face. "Veggies? At a party? What kind of nonsense is that, sugar?"

"Your cardiologist must hate you."

"I'll have you know I'm as fit as a bull."

Beside me, Eddie snorts. "A fat bull."

"Rude."

While those two bicker back and forth, my attention is slowly drawn to the private conversation between Richard and my brother. I can't quite make out what they're saying, their words spoken just under their breath, but if William's frown and pointed gesticulations are anything to go off of, I'm thinking it must be pretty serious.

"What are you two talking about?" I ask.

Richard glances at me and smiles. "This and that."

"Could you be any more vague?"

"We're just talking about the upcoming trial," William explains.

"The logistics of it and all that. It's going to be another couple of months, but who knows how long the trial itself will drag out. We're just discussing living arrangements."

My eyebrows shoot up. "Oh?"

"I'm thinking of getting an apartment," Richard says. "Something a bit more stable and close by. I've got a place in Illinois, but..."

"Why don't you just stay here?" I ask. "The lake house is fine, isn't it?"

"I don't want to overstay my welcome, Win."

"But you're *always* welcome." I turn to look at my brother. "Isn't that right, Will?"

William glances between us, a strange look on his face. His brows are furrowed ever so slightly, his lips pressed into a thin line. *"Win?"* he echoes, sounding almost... weirded out. *"Sugar. Sweetheart. Angel."*

My mouth goes dry. "Oh, uh..."

"You guys need to cool it with the nicknames," William warns. "This is my little sister you're talking to, not your girlfriend. Capisce?"

My heart skips a beat as I cast a nervous glance at Asher. I've been struggling to think of a way to broach the subject, and now feels like as good an opportunity as any. But the words get trapped in the back of my throat and my resolve dwindles and fades far too quickly. It doesn't feel good keeping secrets from my big brother, but this one is *so* big it feels impossible to share.

"William," I begin slowly. "Listen... The guys and I—"

"Last one in the water is a rotten egg!" Eddie shouts, hopping up from his spot on the beach. He reaches for me and throws me over his shoulder, racing toward the lake before I have a chance to protest.

I squeal in delight as we take the plunge together, frankly happy to escape the awkwardness plaguing the moment. I'm surrounded by the cool, refreshing water, a few feet below the surface. The water is dark and a little murky, providing the perfect cover for Eddie to swim up to me and give me a quick kiss before we both swim up for air.

"That was risky," I tease him.

Eddie smiles. "Worth it."

Before we know it, the rest of the guys join us in the water. Richard is quick to throw me onto his shoulders, lifting me up above everyone else. I splash everyone by kicking my feet, initiating an all-out water fight. I lose myself in the laughter, in the smiles, and the warmth of the sun. This is a well-deserved break, the perfect vacation I was hoping for.

Mark my words, this isn't over.

I try to force the colonel's words out of my mind. We're having a good time, and I won't let that horrible man ruin this moment for us. I tell myself he's locked away, secure behind thick concrete and armed guards. There's nothing he can do to hurt us now. All of Asher's heartbreak, Tank's pain, Eddie's suffering, and Richard's stress... It's all over now. It has to be.

But no matter what I do, I can't seem to swallow my doubt.

CHAPTER 26

WINONA

"Get off!"

I shoot out of bed, awake and alert the moment I hear Eddie's terrorized cries. His nightmares haven't gone away—I hadn't expected them to just disappear—and for some reason, they've been getting worse and more frantic.

I burst into his room at the very end of the hall and flip on the light. His eyes are open, but he's not actually cogent. I've seen that look on his face, haunted and horrified. Eddie's in the corner of the room on the floor, curled up on himself.

"Turn off the light," he hisses. "You'll give away our position."

"Eddie," I coo, approaching him as slowly and calmly as I'm able. "Eddie, you need to wake up."

"They've got us surrounded," he rasps. His hand shoots out, so fast it's a blur, and grabs my hand to pull me towards him. "You've got to get out of here. I won't let them hurt you."

"Eddie," I try again. "Eddie, it's just a dream. We're safe. I've got you."

He holds me in his arms, tighter and more secure. Eddie doesn't say anything, but he doesn't have to. When he searches my face, I know he's finally awake because I spot a glimmer of recognition behind his dark eyes. "Winona?"

"Hey, it's okay..."

"Shit, was I dreaming again?"

I give him a small smile. "You were, but it's alright now."

"Did I hurt you?"

Warmth blooms in my chest. Here he is wrestling with his inner demons, and his first and only thought is to make sure *I'm* okay.

"You didn't hurt me," I assure him.

"But I woke you up."

"I'm a light sleeper. If it's not you, then it's Richard's snoring."

Eddie huffs, running a hand through his messy hair. "He does sound like a chainsaw, huh?"

I laugh softly. "You can hear everything through these stupid thin walls."

Out in the hall, the floorboards creak under someone's weight. William is at the door, rubbing sleep from his eyes as he yawns widely.

"What's going on?" he asks. When he sees Eddie and me, he pauses, squinting against the bright light. I suddenly realize how close Eddie and I are, holding onto each other tightly—*too* tightly.

As much as I hate to do it, I let Eddie go and clear my throat. "He was having a bad dream," I explain. "I just wanted to check on him. Make sure everything was okay."

William nods slowly. "You good, Luna?"

Eddie rises from the floor, helping me up along with him. "I'm good. Sorry to disturb your beauty sleep."

"Have you given that therapist I referred to you any more thought?" my brother asks.

"I've got her number." It's not exactly a helpful answer.

I place a hand on Eddie's shoulder. "Look, I... It's probably not my place to tell you, but maybe you should give her a call?"

Everything about his body language screams resistance. His shoulders tense up, his expression sours. I've gotten used to reading all of Eddie's silent cues. When he's happy, he smiles with his eyes, the corners crinkling as he does. When he's upset, he opens and closes his fists, like he's gearing up and readying for a fight. And when he's nervous—just like he is now—he places his weight on one foot and looks like he's getting ready to sprint away from danger.

"You've been having these nightmares for a while now," I say gently, understandingly. "We only want what's best for you. One call can't hurt, right?"

Eddie works his jaw. "I... can't."

"Why not?" William asks, coming off a bit gruff.

I wave him away, warning him with a stern frown. "Why not, Eddie?" I ask again, far more gently.

He swallows hard, Adam's apple bobbing up and down. "I'm not weak."

"No one said you were." I reach down and take his hand without thinking. "You're one of the bravest men I know, Eddie. There's nothing to be embarrassed or ashamed about. All I want is to make sure you're okay, and if talking to someone helps you feel safe and maybe even helps you get better, don't you think that's worth it?"

It takes a moment, but Eddie's breathing eventually calms down. He nods slowly, weighed down by his own weariness. "Okay," he murmurs. "Okay, you're right." He moves like he wants to lean down and kiss me, but we both remember we're not the only ones in the room.

My eyes shift to where my brother is standing. He looks perplexed, to say the least.

"It's late," he says. "We should all be getting to bed."

"Right," I murmur, giving Eddie a quick smile before stepping out into the hall.

My brother casually throws his arm over my shoulder as we head back to our rooms. "What the hell was that all about?" he whispers.

I shrug. "Eddie has nightmares sometimes. PTSD, I think, but I'm no expert."

"No, I mean the way you were looking at each other."

My face flushes with heat, but it's thankfully too dark for him to see. "I don't know what you're talking about."

"Oh, come on, Win. Just now, you guys were..." William sighs. "I don't know. Is something going on between you and Luna?"

Now might be as good a time as any to come clean. I don't feel good about lying to my brother, but I'm a little worried about how he might react. None of this was an issue a few weeks ago when he left me in their care, but that was before we went through hell together. Adversity has made us stronger, the bond I share with all four of the guys too special to put into words. I care for them all deeply, bordering on love...

But if I were in William's shoes, how would I take the news that my little sister is romantically and sexually involved with four of my closest friends? I tell myself William might be understanding and supportive, but I can't assume this will go over smoothly. There's a lot on the line here. Friendships, hearts—I need more time to think about how to tell him. And, at the very least, I should talk with the guys first.

Things feel serious between the four of us, but what are their plans? What do *they* want? They have to stick around after the Fourth of July because of the impending trial, but does that mean they want to continue being with me? On one hand, it makes the butterflies in my stomach flutter thinking about keeping them all to myself. I love the idea of a more serious relationship with all of them, but the only question is *how?*

None of what we have is conventional. It's nice, but it's also strange. In the beginning, I never expected more than a summertime fling, but now? Now I'm not sure if I'm ready to part ways. They all mean too much to me to end things now. Do they feel the same way?

"You're taking way too long to answer," William says, regarding me carefully. "Winona, is something going on? I chew on the inside of my cheek. "No," I lie. It feels *awful*. The word is bitter on my tongue, heavy and deceitful. I just don't know if I'm mentally prepared for what comes next. I tell myself I need a bit more time.

William sighs with relief. "Thank God."

"What do you mean?"

"I respect the man, but I think you can do a lot better."

I frown steeply at this. "Take that back."

"Win—"

"Eddie's a good man, William. I don't understand where this is coming from."

"I never said he wasn't a good man. I just think if you happened to have feelings for him, you should maybe consider... well, *not*. He's clearly got a lot of issues to work through. And I'm not saying it's his fault, but I think you'd be better suited with someone with less... baggage."

A flicker of irritation licks at the back of my neck. "And since when do you weigh in on what happens in my love life?"

"Ever since your shitty, abusive ex-boyfriend."

I cross my arms over my chest. "You're being ridiculous, William. I appreciate your concern, but I'm capable of making my own decisions."

"So there *is* something going on between you and Eddie?"

"I didn't say that. I'm just saying it's not up to you."

"Why are you getting so snippy with me?"

"Because you're—" I cut myself off and take a deep breath. Why *am* I getting so snippy? I understand William's just trying to be protective. Maybe conversations like this shouldn't take place at three in the morning. "Sorry, I'm just tired."

William laughs it off, chuckling softly. "No, you're right. I didn't mean to jump down your throat like that. I probably should have worded it better."

"I'll see you in the morning."

He playfully hits me in the arm. "See you in the morning."

It's almost a relief when I finally get back to the quiet escape of my room. It's chilly in here, and I really wish one of the guys—or all of them, if they felt so inclined—could join me in bed and help warm me up. But it's been increasingly difficult to spend any time alone with them since William is back.

I'm just about to climb under the covers when I notice a draft. My bedroom window is ajar by about half an inch. Strange, considering I don't remember opening it. I make my way over and close it, glancing out at my view of the calm lake. All is tranquil, the silver light of the moon reflecting peacefully off the water's surface.

From behind, someone grabs me.

My scream catches in my throat as the intruder covers my mouth and nose with their hand. Their thick leather gloves make it impossible to draw breath. Panic grips me. I kick and I scratch, but whoever's behind me is too strong for me to fight off. I can't breathe. The edges of my vision start to blur, everything in the room beginning to swim.

"Nothing personal," my attacker huffs against my ear. "Quit struggling. Just go to sleep."

But I don't quit struggling. I continue to fight with every ounce of fleeting strength I have left. I have no clue who this guy is, but I have a sneaking suspicion I know who sent him.

My lungs burn.

My vision goes black.

As unconsciousness drags me under, I can only pray the guys will be safe.

CHAPTER 27

RICHARD

The Fourth of July, a day to celebrate our great country's independence. Fireworks, beer, great food, and even better company... All the building blocks for a wonderful, fun time.

Except festivities are the last thing on my mind.

I'm at the kitchen table, scrolling through the headlines on my laptop while sipping a mug of black coffee. None of the others are up yet. I was tempted to sneak into Winona's room earlier this morning, but given how thin the walls are, I didn't want to risk William overhearing our little rendezvous. Once a Marine, always a Marine, regardless of whether he's retired. There's no doubt in my mind he'll kick my ass if he discovers the truth.

When he discovers the truth.

Because the fact of the matter is I want to tell him. We *all* want to tell him. William deserves our honesty, at the very least. Winona makes me happy, and I know for a fact we all want to make her happy. I know our arrangement is the furthest thing from traditional, but at the end of the day, isn't our happiness all that matters?

There are some people out there who aren't lucky enough to find love. In many ways, I feel like we've won the lottery—finding a girl we can all cherish together. There's nothing to be ashamed of. At least, not in my opinion. The boys and I haven't had a whole lot of time to pull Winona aside to talk to her, but we have every intention of keeping her in our lives. If she'll have us, of course.

I take a large gulp of my coffee and relish the burn as it trickles down my throat, warming my chest and stomach. It's unbelievably bitter, but I like it. Sometimes I'm convinced it's the only proper way to wake up.

I've been scrolling through the same news articles repeatedly, reading every word and drinking up every detail. There haven't been any new developments where Colonel Grey is concerned, but it's only a matter of time before new information comes out. They're supposedly conducting an internal investigation, massive security concerns forcing the higher ups to look into whether he's pulled a stunt like this before. Who knows how many missions, how many *lives,* he's jeopardized before this?

William yawns loudly as he enters the kitchen. "Mornin'."

"You're up early," I say by way of greeting. "Figured all of Eddie's yelling would have disturbed your beauty rest."

"It did, but you know I don't need that many hours of sleep to feel as right as rain." He strides to the counter and helps himself to a mug of coffee. "Winona's not up? She's usually cooking breakfast by the time I'm up and at 'em."

I shrug a shoulder. "She cooks for us out of the kindness of her heart, not because it's her job. She's entitled to a break every now and then."

William chuckles. "Whoa, buddy. I didn't mean anything by it."

I press my lips into a thin line. I wasn't trying to be defensive, but I guess it came across that way. "I didn't mean anything by it, either."

William leans against the counter, mug held just below his chin. He squints at me. "You know... Winona has been kind of..." He shakes his head. "You know what? Never mind."

"What?"

"She's been short with me lately. Acting weird."

"Weird how?" I ask carefully.

"I don't know how to explain it. Just..." He sets his mug down, glancing over his shoulder with a thoughtful frown. "I've been getting a weird feeling."

"That's incredibly vague, Wren. Just tell me."

"What happened between you and my sister while I was away?"

I nearly choke on my coffee. "What?"

"Don't think I haven't noticed," he says flatly. "I thought maybe it's because we've all been through the trenches, but now... I've seen the way you look at her, Wilder. All of you, actually. I tried asking Winona about it last night, but she got all weird on me. And the last couple of days, you've all been acting really..."

"Yes?" I urge.

William takes a deep breath. "I'm going to ask you a question. I want you to answer me honestly. Man to man. No beating around the bush."

I set my mug down and sit back in my chair, steeling myself for what's coming. This certainly wasn't how I expected my morning to go, but William's always been perceptive. He's highly intelligent, and I should have known better than to underestimate him.

"Just ask," I say.

He sets his jaw. "Are you fucking my sister?"

Just as he says this, Tank, Eddie, and Asher all walk in, his question slapping them all across the face.

"Whoa," Tank mumbles awkwardly. "Uh..."

Asher grimaces. "William, listen..."

Eddie doesn't bother sugar coating anything, but then again, it's never been his style. "I guess the cat's finally out of the bag."

William's jaw almost hits the floor. "Seriously? I was *joking!*"

I rub a hand over my face. Jesus Christ, this is a mess.

William's face suddenly turns bright red, rage seeping out of his every pore. "You've got to be kidding me! You're all... Wait, are you fucking serious? *All* of you?"

Tank puts his hands up like he's trying to calm a spooked horse. "Listen, buddy, we can explain—"

"*Winona!*" William shouts for his sister. "Winona, get up right now!"

Asher takes a brave step forward. "Will, let's just take a deep breath—"

"I left her in your care! I trusted you guys to look after her, not... Not *take advantage of her.*"

I rise from my seat. "We didn't take advantage of her."

"A likely story!" William seethes. "A young, vulnerable woman— Seriously, all *four* of you? Fuck, did you... Did you guys force her to—"

"That is not what happened," Eddie snaps back. "Who do you think we are? We'd never do something like that."

"This was a consensual relationship between adults," Asher says calmly, diplomatically. "Nobody did anything they didn't want to."

I approach cautiously, more than a little aware of the veins in William's temple threatening to burst. "We care for her deeply, Will. We have no intention of hurting Winona."

"Care for her deeply," he echoes in disbelief. "What do you... *love* her?"

None of us answer. Truth be told, it might be a little too early to be throwing the L-word around, but one look at my friends and I can tell we're all well on our way there. Unfortunately, our silence doesn't help our case.

"You assholes!" William exclaims. "With my *sister?* Do you take turns or—Actually, fuck. I don't want to know."

"We're not just fooling around," Tank says. "What we have with Winona... It's special."

"Like hell!" he roars before storming off down the hall. We all give chase, an anxious energy passing between us. "Winona!" William bellows, hammering his fists against her door. "Winona, get up this instant!"

"You need to calm down," I warn, following him.

"Don't fucking tell me what to do. Winona—"

When his fist next meets the door, it swings open slowly on its weak hinges. My first and only concern is to protect Winona at all cost. I'm confident William would never hurt her, but I don't like the idea of her being confronted so early in the morning—or, frankly, at all.

Her bed is empty.

She's nowhere in sight.

We look around her room in confusion, taking in the destruction.

The open window. Her bed sheets in a tangle. Books and photographs tossed around like a tornado had come through. I'm no detective, but I know the signs of a kidnapping when I see one. And the little note William finds nestled on her pillow only solidifies my theory.

"What does it say?" Eddie asks gruffly.

William's eyes scan over the words. "*If you want her back alive, come to the address listed below. Come unarmed. If you involve the police, we'll kill her and dump her body where you'll never find it.*"

CHAPTER 28

WINONA

There's no point in crying or freaking out. I'll have plenty of time for that later. Right now, I need to figure out where the hell I am and how to get out.

I come to in the back of a gutted moving van, my wrists bound behind my back and my ankles bound with thick zip ties. Someone has slapped a long strip of duct tape over my mouth to keep me from screaming. There's no telling how much time has passed because the windows have all been spray painted black, banishing any light from streaming in.

Has it been a few minutes? Hours? Days? Who knows?

Just as I start to wriggle around on the van floor, my left foot knocks into something hard and solid. I fold in on myself to try and get a better look, but it's too dark to see anything. All I've got to work with is the faint red glow of a small LCD screen that reads: *UNARMED.*

Unarmed? What the hell am I looking at right now?

The more I shuffle around on the van floor, the more I bump into other hard blocks. I'm surrounded. There's barely any space to move.

Closing my eyes, I listen carefully. I can just make out the muffled sounds of conversation. Music. Distant fireworks. Someone outside is talking. I think they're close. Maybe if I scream, they'll hear me. The tape over my mouth makes it next to impossible, but I refuse to give up. I stretch my jaw and manage to wet the sticky side with my spit, slowly but surely loosening the tape from my face. When the corner finally peels away, I start screaming.

"Help!" I scream with every ounce of strength I can muster. "Someone help me! Is anybody there?"

Suddenly, the back doors of the van swing open. A mix of moonlight and the orange glow of streetlights floods into the cramped space, giving me enough light to see what the hell is going on.

I freeze, my breath catching in my throat.

Bombs. I'm surrounded by an entire stockpile of C4 wired to a single trigger and display. It's a rat's nest of blue, red, and black wires, weaving in and around the blocks of C4 like writhing snakes. I don't know the first thing about explosives, but even I know there's enough here to destroy the entire neighborhood. One wrong move might set the whole thing off.

"Don't worry," a low, dark voice murmurs. "Nothing's going to happen as long as you're a good little girl and do as I say."

I glare up at the shadowy figure standing on the other side of the van doors. Most of his face is cast in shadow, but I'd recognize that heartless voice and hulking figure anywhere.

"How the hell did you get out of jail?" I hiss through gritted teeth. "I was convinced you'd rot in there until your court date."

The colonel shrugs casually, looking down his long nose with his usual air of disdain. "You forget who I am, Ms. Wren. I have many friends in high places."

"Rats, you mean. You're going to pay for this."

"Save your speeches. I have no interest in hearing them."

"When the guys find out I'm missing, they'll tear you to shreds. They won't stop until they find me."

"I'm counting on it, my dear."

It takes a moment for my concussed brain to realize what he's talking about. The colonel *wants* the guys to come after me because...

"You're going to kill them. And you're using me as bait."

"Would you like to state anything else obvious? Perhaps next you'll tell me the sky is blue and water is wet."

My lip curls up into a sneer. "Actually, asshole, water isn't wet. Wetness is just a description of our experience of water."

The colonel snorts. "Semantics."

"What exactly is your plan here?" I snap. "You'll lure them here to me, but I'm sure they'll realize something's off. I'll warn them about the bombs."

"You won't be able to after I've carved out your tongue."

My eyes widen in pure horror. "You wouldn't."

"Continue to test me and we'll see."

"Get the fuck away from you, you monster!" I frantically glance over his shoulder, trying to look for something—anything—that might help me get out of here.

I see no people, but I can hear them. There's loud music playing, joyous conversation, the occasional firework going off. If I had to venture a guess, I think I'm somewhere near water. Just past his shoulder, I can see the harbor. The fishy waters of the bay flood my nose, the distant call of seagulls floating into my ear. I'm pretty sure the colonel's parked us somewhere downtown right in the middle of Fourth of July celebrations!

My heart plummets into the pit of my stomach. If the bombs go off, how many innocent people will be hurt? Men, women, and children—*families.*

"Why did it have to be here?" I rasp. "How can you be so heartless?"

"It's a contingency, my dear." The colonel leans against the doors casually, his arms splayed out like a hawk about to dive in for the kill. "I can't just target the men. That'll be too obvious. I need this to look like an accident."

Air rushes out of my lungs. "An accident?"

"That's correct, Ms. Wren. A Fourth of July mishap. When these bombs go off—and they will the moment one of your boys tries to open the door—people will think it was a fireworks show gone wrong. It'll take the police a while to parse together what really happened, and by then, I'll be long gone. It's the perfect cover."

"What about Asher?" I scream. It's my last Hail Mary to try and get this lunatic to see reason. "You'd really kill your own grandson? You should have heard the way he tried to defend you when Richard expressed his suspicions! He admires and respects you so much. How could you do this to him?"

"If that's really what he thinks, then I raised a fool. The only person you should ever trust is yourself."

I realize there's no point in trying to reason with the colonel. This man is a lost cause, so wrapped up in his greed and cruelty his heart can't possibly be swayed. In many ways, I see Chet in him. Self-centered. Egotistical. An all-around dickhead. I'd rather not waste any more of my precious time—what little I might have left—trying to change the man's mind.

"I'd better get going," the colonel says, daring to toss me a wink. "Settle in, Ms. Wren. Try not to move too much. C4 is *very* sensitive. One tiny bump and you'll blow yourself sky high."

I tense when the colonel slams the door shut, locking me inside as he laughs darkly. He must have some sort of remote because the display suddenly flicks from *UNARMED* to *ARMED*.

The air is too thin to breathe. Every fiber of my being is on the brink of tearing. I have so much tension in my body I'm surprised my spine hasn't snapped into two. I can't afford to panic when there's so much on the line. I struggle against my bindings, ignoring the sharp bite of the zip ties as they chew into the skin of my wrists. Something feels sticky. I wonder if I'm bleeding. I'm honestly not surprised when I catch the faint hint of iron lingering in the air.

I'm not ready to give up, though. Not by a long shot. I can't rely on the guys to save me this time, because saving me means I'll have led them right to their deaths. I need to figure this out on my own—or die trying. I cannot, and will not, let my men get hurt because of me.

I continue to struggle, twisting my wrists back and forth, side to side. The entire time, I keep telling myself it's just plastic. Sturdy as it may be, everything eventually gives. At this point, it's only a matter of willpower. No matter how much this hurts, no matter how much pain I have to endure, I keep going until I finally hear a snap.

The zip tie head tears off, freeing my wrists. My shoulders ache and my wrists throb, but there's no time to relish the relief. Not when I'm surrounded by explosives that could go off at any moment.

I think about what the colonel said. This entire van is rigged to blow the second someone opens the door. Even if it weren't, I can't just leave thousands of pounds of C4 in the middle of the busy downtown core amidst unsuspecting partygoers. It's too dangerous to abandon, so I need to take it somewhere out of range of civilians.

Reaching down, I hastily pry off the zip ties binding my legs together. It's a trial and a half, and I end up accidentally kicking my leg out and bumping one of the blocks of C4. Blessedly nothing happens. Quickly but carefully, I hop up onto my hands and knees and feel around in the dark, making my way to the front seat of the van.

I can see the harbor better from here. The van is parked on the hill, which I think I can use to my advantage. The colonel was too smart to leave the keys or any spares inside the van, but that's no matter. Even without a running engine, I can still jam the gear shift into neutral and let gravity take care of the rest.

And hopefully not plow into anybody on the way down.

My heart races as the van lurches forward. I've got both my feet on the brake, doing my best to keep the vehicle from losing control. It's difficult to turn the wheel, but I narrowly manage to avoid parked cars and pedestrians. I lay on the horn, frantically gesturing at people to get the hell out of my way.

I crank the window down, but only an inch. Wires are everywhere, connection pieces at the windows and the door itself. I don't know the first thing about circuitry, but something tells me if these connections come apart, it'll set the C4 off.

"Move!" I shout out the crack of the window. "Runaway van! Move it!"

People's reactions vary. Some flip me off, others watch in curiosity and amusement, while others look downright concerned. If only they knew this thing is equipped with enough firepower to blow up the entire harbor, they'd probably run scared—and for good reason.

I let the slope of the hill guide me forward. I have neither a destination nor a plan in mind. Surely anywhere is better than here, but *where?*

"Think, Winona, think!"

I continue to lay on the horn, but the crowd is becoming denser. People flip me off, yelling at me as the van plows through the area. It's frankly a miracle I haven't hit anyone yet, but it's only a matter of time.

"Watch where you're going!"

"What the fuck are you doing, you crazy bitch?"

"I'm sorry!" I scream out the window.

Up ahead, I see them.

Asher, Tank, Eddie, Richard, and William.

They came for me, but I'm the furthest thing from relieved. Knowing them, they'll try and rip me out of the van. But the second these doors open...

Tank waves his good arm over his head. "There she is! Winona, over here—"

"Get out of the way!" I screech and zip right by them.

CHAPTER 29

TANK

"Get out of the way!"

The van careens forward with no signs of stopping, people ahead scattering left and right to avoid collision. Instinctively, we chase after Winona, confusion swirling between us.

"What the hell is going on?" Eddie shouts.

"We have to catch her!" Asher bellows.

So we run, chasing the white van with tinted black windows. From the way it jerks and pulls, I don't think Winona has complete control. The van is going fast enough it's starting to cause a bit of a panic amongst celebrators, but not so fast we can't catch it. The five of us gain enough speed and traction to catch up to it, shouting at people to get out of the way while desperately trying to get to Winona.

Asher, arguably the fastest of us, manages to catch up to the vehicle first. He's just about to pull on the door handle when Winona screams, "No! Don't!"

He grips the side mirror. "What's going on? Stop the—"

"I can't stop! There's a massive bomb back here. If you open the doors, it'll go off!"

"Fuck," I hiss. "Is the colonel nearby?"

"I don't know!" she says around a sob, tears staining her cheeks. I can't imagine her terror. "You guys have to get away. He's using me to get to you!"

"We're not leaving you!" Eddie exclaims, catching up on the other side.

The situation is growing more and more dire. If the colonel is close, there's a chance he might be able to trigger the bomb remotely. Not ideal, given how many civilians could become collateral damage.

I look out to the bay, observing the water. There are only a few boats out right now because of the scheduled fireworks show over the water. An idea hits me.

"We need to ditch the van in the bay!" I shout.

"My sister's still inside, you idiot!" William hisses.

"We'll pull her out once we've got the whole thing submerged," Richard explains without missing a beat. "If the bomb goes off, the water will absorb most of the shock."

"Are we forgetting about the part where Winona's trapped inside?"

"When the water pressure evens out, we'll break the windshield and yank her out. It's the only way! You got that, Winona?"

She gulps hard, but nods all the same, worry twisting her pretty face.

"It's going to be okay, sugar," I say. "We got you. We're not going to let anything else happen to you. Now, *steer*."

The end of the dock is coming up, more and more people gathering around to watch the chaos unfold even though that's the exact opposite of what we want.

"Stay back!" Asher shouts. "Evacuate the area immediately!"

"You heard the man!" Richard snaps. "Get out of here! This thing's going to blow!"

At this, people finally come to their senses and disperse. Some of them are calm about it, vacating the area as safely as possible. Others... Not so much. They run and scream, their chaotic reaction inciting a frenzy. We can't worry about that right now, though, because the end of the dock is coming up.

Eight yards.

Six yards.

Four.

Two.

"Brace yourselves!" Winona shouts out the window.

The van goes first, plunging beneath the dark and murky waters. It's nothing short of a miracle that the impact didn't jostle the bomb hard enough to detonate. Contrary to what people might expect thanks to the movies and television, the vehicle doesn't immediately plummet to the bottom of the bay. Instead, it's a mildly rapid sink, water rushing in to engulf the insides.

My friends and I don't hesitate. We're in the water, latching on as it goes down, down, *down*... It's a rush of air bubbles, of filtered lights and fireworks above. Disorienting. It's next to impossible to see down here. Time is of the essence—as is the air in our lungs. We need to make this fast or we all might drown.

Eddie is the first to the windshield, hammering it with his fists with unmatched ferocity. It's no small feat, either. Throwing a punch under water is almost three times as hard as on land because of the additional resistance. And while he makes it look easy, the windshield just won't give.

We're all the way at the bottom now, the tires sinking into the cold grip of the sand. There's next to no light down here. We're working by touch, running on intuition. The seconds are counting down. Any number of things could go wrong. We could run out of air. The bomb could go off.

Winona could drown. She could *die*.

The thought chills me to the bone. I won't let that happen. I can't. If anything happens to her, I'll tear the colonel's throat out and see him personally to Hell. Feeling around at the bottom, I search for something—anything—sharp and hard enough to give us a leg up. My hand bumps against something solid. A rock. Jagged with a pointed tip, and heavy enough to give enough leverage.

I swim over. Eddie and I are already so in tune he has his hand outstretched, ready to receive the impromptu tool. He brings the point down on the windshield, the glass cracking a little. He tries again, applying more pressure. This does the trick. In the blink of an eye, the windshield shatters into a thousand impossible shards.

There's no time to think. I reach out and grab Winona, pulling her toward me. I don't think she's conscious. We need to get her to the surface—and fast.

The only problem is I'm running out of steam. I can feel it in the weight of my legs, in the burn of my lungs, in the blurry edges of my vision. How long have we been down here? A few seconds? Five minutes? Did I take a big enough breath before diving in? Shit, the surface is so far away. Why can't I swim any faster?

Richard swoops in, taking Winona with him in his arms while William gives me a helpful push. They've always been the strongest, so it's no surprise their strength applies to their swimming capabilities, as well.

The first thing I do when I reach the top is take a huge gulp of crisp air. I think I hear Asher shout something about getting to shore, but I have no sweet clue. Not with all this water clogging up my ears. I swim in the same direction as them, eager to check on Winona.

Her eyes are closed.

I don't think she's breathing.

Richard drags her onto the embankment, checking her over. "Come on, sweetheart. Wake up." He presses his ear to her chest, comes away with a wide-eyed horror. The panic doesn't last long, though, because he immediately begins administering CPR.

And all I can do—all *any* of us can do—is watch.

A minute feels like an eternity. Out of the corner of my eye, I see the red and blue flash of emergency vehicle lights. Help is on the way, but it isn't fast enough. I'm not a praying man. Never really have been. But in this moment, I pray like I've never prayed before.

I don't know what I'll do if Winona doesn't make it. I need her. *We* need her. Until now, Winona has felt like an inevitability. Since she walked into our lives, we were always meant to be together. The five of us, happy and content. I can't possibly imagine a future without her. Now that she's slipping from our grasp—I can't stand it. I can't stand it at all.

"Come on," I mutter. "Please, Winona."

Richard tries everything. Chest compressions. Pinching her nose and blowing into her mouth. Nothing's working. Just when I'm about to lose hope—

She gasps, back arching and her head tilting back as water trickles from her lips. Winona coughs the water out, breathing shakily as she clutches onto Richard, and then Asher, and then Eddie, and then me. We hold her like our lives depend on it, cradling her and showing her we're here, that it's all going to be okay.

"We got you," Asher says against her cheek, pressing a kiss to her pale skin. "We got you, angel."

Once she's regained some semblance of calm, the first thing she asks is, "Are any of you hurt? Please tell me none of you are—"

"We're fine, sweetheart," Eddie says. "Totally fine."

"The bomb?"

"At the bottom of the bay," Richard explains. "We'll still need a bomb squad to disarm it, though. It's too much of a risk to leave it down there."

"And the colonel?"

I shake my head. "We haven't seen him. But we'll hunt him down as soon as we get you to the hospital."

"No." William's voice is hard. "I'll take her to the hospital. You four need to get that son of a bitch."

We all nod. As much as we want to stay with Winona, we're all thinking the same thing. The colonel isn't going to get away this time. After all the shit he's put us through, it's time to end this —permanently.

CHAPTER 30

EDDIE

We're ready this time.

After grabbing our supplies out of the trunk, we split into teams of two. There are no instructions given, no orders spoken. We're a well-oiled machine, so attuned with one another that communication is unnecessary.

Our mission is loud and clear: find the colonel.

Bring him in.

And this time, make sure he doesn't escape.

We have a lot of ground to cover, but he can't have gotten very far given the fact that he had to be here in person to arm the bomb in the back of the van. I team up with Richard, while Asher and Tank split off together.

There are too many moving parts. Lots of partygoers—some disoriented in their celebratory drunkenness—ebbing and flowing like the crowd has a pulse of its own. A living, breathing organism we must wade through. My boots are still sopping wet, moisture dripping from the ends of my hair, but there's no time to squirm in the uncomfortable sensation. Right now, I need to scan the endless sea of faces, sift through this haystack to find a single needle.

I spot him a few blocks away. I can just make out the shape of his back and a tuft of his hair, but I know it's him.

"There!" I shout at Richard.

We're on the move, forcing our way through the crowded streets with our weapons tucked away. I've got a knife in my boot, a pistol in my jacket's inner pocket, and another handgun tucked into the back of my waistband.

Do I need this much firepower to take on an old man? No.

Do I *want* to use this much firepower to take on an old man? Fuck, yes.

He may be a few yards ahead, but we have the advantage of speed and stamina. I don't see anyone with him, but I'm not about to let my guard down. The colonel has proven himself more slippery than an eel. Someone must have helped him escape jail. And not just any jail, but military prison. I wouldn't be surprised if—

All of a sudden, a man comes barreling out from around the corner. He tackles me to the ground with a mighty roar, his fist slamming into my jaw. Pain radiates outward, but instead of letting it stun me, I use it as fuel. All at once, I'm enraged. I think about my brothers who I couldn't save. I think about my brothers who I *can* save. One lucky punch is all I'm going to afford this asshole. It's time for some overdue payback.

I swiftly bring my knee up and nail him in the groin. He squeaks pathetically, stumbling back as he tries to draw in a breath. I lunge at him before he gets the chance to stabilize, throwing him hard against the nearby wall of a building. A swift roundhouse kick to the jaw knocks him out cold. I think I hear a couple of his teeth crack. Excellent.

"Keep moving!" Richard orders before the guy's body even has a chance to slump to the ground. "There's more ahead!"

I grimace. I should have known it wouldn't be easy.

There are five of them. If Asher and Tank were here, at least the odds would be somewhat more even. But they're not, and I'm frankly thankful for the challenge. I have all this pent-up rage and energy bottled up inside me, and it's about fucking time I let loose.

One, two, three. I take them all at once. A punch, a kick, a throw. My knuckles crack, my shoulders pop. It's pretty clear I'm not as young as I used to be, but I still have the same fighting spirit. One of my attackers tries drawing their weapon, but I don't let them. I react before he has a chance to fire a bullet, ramming my shoulder against his ribcage so hard he wheezes. I disarm him in the blink of an eye before hitting him across the back of the skull with the butt of his own gun.

I clap my hands clean as I watch Richard take care of the last two men.

"Show off," he huffs. His brow is covered in sweat.

I smirk. "Try and keep up."

"The colonel?"

"This way."

We're gaining on him. I think he knows it, too, because he takes a sharp turn around a corner and disappears from sight. We chase after him, elbowing past bystanders while ignoring their jeers and scoffs.

Up ahead, a waiting car. The coward is trying to flee. Not on my watch.

As soon as I'm sure no civilians are in the way, I draw my pistol and aim for the tires. My aim is true, the loud *bang bang* of the front and back tires ringing loud and clear. The colonel is forced to abandon his escape vehicle, dashing down a narrow alley. He stops at the end, closed-off with nowhere to go.

We've got him.

Asher and Tank catch up to us, their weapons already drawn.

The colonel looks at Asher. "Dear boy, let's talk about this—"

Asher lifts his dart gun, loaded with a powerful tranquilizer strong enough to take down a horse. With all of Tank's connections from the farm, it was easy to grab a dose last-minute for this exact purpose.

"Shut up, asshole," Asher grumbles before pulling the trigger.

The dart hits his grandfather square in the chest. The effects of the drug are immediate. The colonel's knees give out first, wobbly and unstable. His whole body goes limp not long after as he falls to the side, his eyes drifting closed, his mouth still wide open in surprise. He'll live, unfortunately. This is frankly too merciful an end for my liking, but I should have expected as much. Asher may hate the man as much as we do now, but he's not going to murder his own grandfather in cold blood.

He's too good of a man to stoop that low.

We all are.

CHAPTER 31

WINONA

The doctors and nurses run all sorts of tests on me. Apparently, blacking out due to lack of oxygen twice within the span of twenty-four hours is considered pretty bad news. I know I'm in good hands here, but I'm so anxious.

"Have you heard anything from the guys yet?" I ask my brother for the millionth time. "We'd know if something happened by now, right?"

William sighs. "Relax, Win. I'm sure they've got everything under control. They're professionals, remember?"

I squirm against the scratchy hospital sheets. This is by far the most uncomfortable bed I've lain in in a very long time. They've got me hooked up to all sorts of monitoring equipment, a strap around my arm and chest, and even an oxygen tube wrapped around my face and plugged into my nose. I personally think it's overkill because I feel perfectly fine.

William takes a seat in the guest chair beside my hospital bed, leaning against the frame's railing with his fingers locked together before him. He studies me intently, lips pressed into a thin, contemplative line.

"I need to ask you a question," he says.

"What?"

"You'll have to forgive me for being so abrupt, but I don't think it can wait. My curiosity has been eating me alive."

I settle in bed, thinking I probably know what he's curious about. "What is it, Will?"

He looks... uncomfortable. I think that's the best way to describe it. Like he's searching his mind for the right words, but they elude him at every turn. It takes him a minute to muster up the courage to ask, "The guys... How do you feel about them?"

"I don't understand."

"Do you love them?"

The silence that falls over us is thick and heavy. I suppose there's no point in trying to lie.

"Yes," I answer softly. "I love them very much."

"*All* of them?"

I nod, steadfast and sure. "Asher, Tank, Eddie, and Richard... I love them. I know that's probably not what you want to hear, and it's probably difficult to understand, but it's the truth. Those men have my heart."

William stiffens, but he doesn't lose his composure. "I see," he answers slowly. "And I'm assuming this means..."

"We've been intimate, yes."

I don't blame my brother for the way he cringes, but that's honestly the most delicate way of putting it.

"Please," I say, "don't be upset with them. I'm the one who crossed the line. I know they're some of your closest friends and I should have respected that boundary, but things happened so quickly..."

"I saw the way they looked at you. When they pulled you out of the water. For a moment there, I thought we might have lost you."

"I'm sorry. I didn't mean to give you all a scare."

William takes a deep breath. "You should have seen the looks on their faces, Win. If you hadn't made it..." He chuckles, shaking his head slightly. "I'm convinced the guys would have burned the world down for you."

My eyes sting with the threat of tears. "I have no doubt they would."

"Are you happy? Being with them."

I nod, a smile spreading across my lips at the mere thought of my men. "So happy." I reach over and place my hand gently over my brother's. "I know this is strange. I'm sure people might not approve—"

"Nobody else's opinion matters, Win."

His comment takes me by surprise. "Not even yours?"

William runs a hand through his hair and huffs. "Look, it's... weird. And I'm definitely going to need some time to get used to the idea. A *long* time to get used to the idea. I just don't want to see you get hurt, that's all."

"I won't," I promise. "The guys would never hurt me."

"I know. They're all honorable, good men. I trusted them with my life when we fought overseas, and I guess I trust them with your life, too."

I sit up a little straighter. "Wait, are you giving me your blessing?"

William laughs. "Not that you need it to begin with, but yeah."

I lean over and pull him into a tight hug. "Thank you, Will."

He rubs my back. "You're welcome, Win."

"Where is she?" a booming voice fills the emergency room triage. Asher. "I want to see her."

"Sir," an exasperated nurse says quickly, "please lower your voice. I'm afraid only family can visit right now."

William pokes his head out from behind the privacy curtain surrounding my little hospital bed. "They *are* family," he says, waving them over.

Asher, Tank, Eddie, and Richard file into the small space, making it even more cramped than it was, but I honestly can't say I mind. They're quick to spoil me with tender hugs and sweet kisses, the love in their eyes undeniable.

"Did you get him?" I ask.

Asher nods. "Yes. He's been detained and transported to a high-security facility."

"They're moving his trial up to the end of next week" Tank explains, "because he's such a flight risk."

"How are you feeling, sweetheart?" Eddie asks, holding onto my hand like it's some sort of lifeline. I adore the way he rubs his thumb over my knuckles, so gentle and caring it makes me want to cry.

"I'm alright," I tell them. "The doctors won't let me go yet, though. Not until I get my test results back. I'm not too sure what they're looking for."

"Better safe than sorry," Richard says, seated at the edge of my bed. He has a protective hand on my shin.

"Thank you all for saving me," I mumble. "I don't know what I would have done without you."

Asher tucks a strand of my hair behind my ear. "There's nothing to thank us for. We're always going to protect you. We love you."

I smile so wide my cheeks start to feel sore. An uncontrollable warmth blooms in my chest. "I love you all, too."

William, being William, shudders. "Ugh."

"Problem, Wren?" Eddie asks coyly.

"Can you guys tone down the lovey-dovey stuff? Just because I'm okay with you being with my sister doesn't mean I want it rubbed in my face."

"You mean like this?" Tank asks as he cups my cheeks in his hands and plants a wet, hot kiss on my lips. I laugh into it, sighing contently.

My brother makes a face. "I'm going to fucking deck you."

The privacy curtain pulls to the side before he can make good on his threat. A doctor in a crisp white lab coat steps in with a clipboard in hand. She glances at the five gargantuan men standing around me and blushes.

"O-oh my," she stutters. "Looks like we've got ourselves a full house."

"How's she doing?" Eddie asks, wasting no time. "Is she free to go yet?"

"Soon," the doctor promises. "I just wanted to talk to you about your results. Would you like a little privacy, or..."

"They can stay," I reply. "I want them to."

"Alright." She clears her throat and flips through a couple of pages. "All in all, everything's looking good. There's nothing to be overly concerned about. However, I would like to keep you overnight to keep an eye on the baby and—"

"Whoa, what?"

"Excuse me?"

"What was that?"

All of them speak at once.

The poor doctor smiles at them. "Oh, uh... We did some blood work on Ms. Wren. It's showing higher than usual levels of hCG—the pregnancy hormone. She's a couple of weeks along, give or take."

My jaw drops. "I'm—"

William rises from his seat, putting his hands up in the air. "I'm going to... Yeah, I'm going to go before I throttle someone."

I ignore him. "I don't understand. I haven't felt any symptoms."

The doctor nods. "Some women can feel them as early as a few weeks, some after about a month. It varies from person to person."

A sudden wave of bliss and elation washes over me. *Pregnant.* I'll admit I haven't given much thought about having children or starting a family, but this feels right in a way I can't even begin to put into words. I already feel so protective of the baby growing in my belly. There's no doubt in my mind that plans for my future will have to change, but I'm ready.

I look around the small space and take in everyone's expressions. The guys all look over the moon.

Richard is the first to give me a reassuring nod. "We got you," he says, and that's all I really need to hear. I have no idea what motherhood is going to bring, but as long as I have them by my side, I'm prepared to take on the world.

EPILOGUE

WINONA

September

New York is an absolute dream.

We really lucked out apartment-wise, nabbing a spacious five-bedroom apartment with a garden terrace and a gorgeous kitchen. There's plenty of light and high ceilings, so it feels like I can really, truly thrive here. Of course, the five of us only ever use my bedroom, but I'm not complaining. After the trial, the guys decided to retire from the military and are now in the process of starting a security business together. Luckily, all four of them have invested most of their earnings in highly profitable startups, like William's, so they have easy cash flow.

"Good job summarizing those editorial notes," Nancy says as she passes my desk. "Can you forward me a copy when you email the author?"

I nod and smile. "Absolutely."

"Thanks, Winona. You're the best." Nancy leans against the edge of my workstation with a coy smile. "I read the first ten pages of your manuscript, by the way. Talk about a sizzling romance!"

"You really like it?"

"Are you kidding? I need the full manuscript, *stat*. I know you're only here for a short time as an intern, but there's no rule against taking you on as an author."

My cheeks flush with warmth. I'll admit the only reason I started writing was to recount everything that happened to me over the summer. Obviously, I changed names and the setting, but it was always meant for my own amusement. When Nancy saw me working on my story a few weeks ago, she all but begged me to send it her way. I'll confess the idea of being a published author is kind of thrilling.

"Thanks, Nancy. That means a lot. I've only got a few more chapters to finish, but I can send the pages to you by the end of the week."

Nancy squeals. "I can't wait! I need to know if Penelope chooses Adam, Terrance, Evan, or Rhys." She pumps her eyebrows suggestively. "Or is this more of a *no need to choose* kind of love story?"

I shrug, giving her a coy smirk. "I guess you'll have to read it to find out."

The rest of my day goes by quickly. I'm really enjoying my work here as an intern. There's so much going on and so much to learn. Between reading through agent query letters, getting my hands on fresh manuscripts, and drafting standard literary contracts, it's never a dull day working for a major publishing house.

By the time my workday is over and I'm walking through the front exit, I find Richard waiting for me on the sidewalk. He offers his elbow with a charming smile.

"How was work today?"

I give him a kiss and quickly hook my arm through his. "It was wonderful! Nancy wants to read the rest of my manuscript."

"I told you she would, didn't I?"

I giggle. "Yes, I was wrong to doubt you. I thought Eddie was picking me up today? Not that I'm complaining, of course."

"He texted me to say his therapy session was running a bit long," Richard explains. "So I volunteered to escort you home."

"You know I'm perfectly capable of taking the train home by myself, right?"

His eyes flick down to my belly. I'm only three months along, but my belly is *just* starting to show. "I'd rather not risk it. Do you have any idea what the crime rate is?"

I laugh. "You're such a worrywart."

Richard presses a kiss to the top of my head. "And for good reason. Nothing's more precious to me than you and the little one."

I love our routine of domesticity.

Eddie and I often cook together, spending our lazy afternoons baking up a storm. Asher and I have begun arranging one of the bedrooms into a nursery for our little one, flipping through catalogs and debating which color we should paint the walls. Tank likes to take me out on long walks through Central Park where we can gaze at the flowers, trees, and local wildlife. And Richard has made it his personal mission to dote on me hand and foot, never once complaining about late-night food runs whenever my wild cravings strike.

My favorite thing to do is laze around in bed with them on Sunday mornings, wrapped up in so many strong arms and legs I think I might overheat. I adore the little things, like the way Tank sometimes talks in his sleep, or the way Richard snores so loudly I'm worried one of our neighbors will file a noise complaint, or the way Eddie and Asher always seem to wrestle in their sleep while fighting over who gets to hold me.

But this particular Sunday morning, I get up before the rest of them, turning the envelope I received in the mail over and over \ in my hand. The morning sun lifts over the horizon, painting the inside of our apartment a gorgeous wash of orange, pink, and gold. I've got the coffee machine going, but it's not for me. I've discovered the easiest way to wake my men up is by making the whole place smell of coffee.

Asher is the first one up. He rubs sleep from his eyes. "Are you okay, angel?"

I glance up at him and nod, smiling gently. "Everything's fine."

Eddie is the next out of bed. He stretches his arms over his head, yawning wide like a lion in the savannah. "Good morning, sweetheart. What do you have there?"

I nibble on my bottom lip, hesitant. "The paternity test results. The doctor sent them over last night, but I didn't want to open it yet."

"Oh," he mumbles, joining me at the kitchen table. Eddie places a loving kiss to the back of my neck.

Tank and Richard are next. Both shirtless, both gorgeous as sin with their messy hair and wide chests. But their puffy eyes and the sleep lines against their cheek make them nothing short of adorable. I'm about to open my mouth to explain, but Richard nods.

"We heard."

Now that we've all gathered at the table, I hold the envelope out to Asher. "Do you want to do the honors?"

He shakes his head. "I don't think I want to know."

"You don't?"

"I'm going to love you and the baby as my own all the same," he explains kindly. "The results aren't going to change how I treat you or the child."

Tank, Eddie, and Richard all nod. "Us, too."

"I think you should hold onto it," Tank suggests. "For when the kid asks."

I hold my breath, looking at each one of them with love and awe. "Okay. Sounds like a plan."

Richard leans over to press a kiss to the top of my hair. "Now, what's in the second envelope?" he asks. "The one you're hiding under the placemat."

I laugh. "Nothing gets by you, does it?"

"Rarely."

I switch the envelopes out, the second one marked *Gender Reveal* in the doctor's looping handwriting. I hold it up and grin. "Who wants to know if we're having a boy or a girl? Or both?" I add with a little laugh.

Tank looks like he's about to fly out of his chair. "Should I be sitting for this? I feel like I should be sitting for this."

"I bet we get two boys," Eddie says.

"Care to make a wager?" Asher jokes.

"A hundred million dollars."

"I'm assuming that's in Monopoly money?" Richard chides.

"I think it's going to be girls," Asher says.

"We might get one of each," Richard adds.

"Go on, sugar. Open it."

I rip into the envelope, my heart racing. I take the sheet of paper inside and carefully unfold it, my eyes scanning the words. I can barely contain my excitement when I say, "We're having a boy *and* a girl!"

There are cheers and hugs and kisses all around. My joy knows no bounds. There's no doubt in my mind my children will be surrounded by love and light, with four strong protectors watching out for them every step of the way.

The End

Printed in Great Britain
by Amazon